"I should go..."

Jamie turned to Maya, brow furrowed. "Why?"

"Because of what just happened. I don't think—"

Jamie reached over and touched her cheek. "Maya, stop. Us sleeping together won't be a problem unless we let it be one. And what happened here tonight doesn't have to follow us back home and into the office."

She took a deep breath. She was relieved that it wouldn't put a strain on their working relationship, but also crestfallen that this wouldn't go anywhere beyond this one night.

"We're both adults," he continued. "And I think we both needed to finally get that out of our systems before we imploded. Don't you think?"

"Yes, I do." She had spent too many waking, and sleeping, hours lusting over this man.

Her *boss*.

Dear Reader,

I'm going to be honest, I'm pretty new to the world of romance. It was during a province-wide blackout in December 2013 when I read my first romance novel. My phone's battery was full and I decided to buy ebooks to kill some time. While my friends played a board game, I searched for something to read, and I happened upon the romance section of the online store and came across some Harlequin Blaze titles. By the time the power came back on, I had finished six books. I was hooked!

One thing that attracted me to Harlequin Blaze was its strong, feisty heroines. A Blaze heroine has her own life, a successful career, an unbreakable, independent spirit, and—at first—she needs nothing from the hero...except for a few wild nights, that is. I admired that and much more about the classic Blaze heroine, and I kept that in mind as I wrote Maya.

Getting *In the Boss's Bed* from my mind into your hands, dear reader, has been an amazing journey. This is my first book, and I hope you enjoy reading about Maya and Jamie as much as I enjoyed creating them.

Cheers!

Juanita

J. Margot Critch

In the Boss's Bed

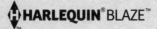

Recycling programs
for this product may
not exist in your area.

ISBN-13: 978-0-373-79902-2

In the Boss's Bed

Printed in U.S.A.

Juanita Margot Critch currently lives in St. John's, Newfoundland, with her husband, Brian, and their two little buddies, Simon and Chibs. She spends equal amounts of time writing, listening to Jimmy Buffett's music and looking out at the ocean, all the while trying to decide if she wants coffee or a margarita.

For Mom. You've always been my biggest fan and supporter, no matter what wacky thing I'm up to. I love you.

And Brian, my fierce, loyal, alpha-protector with beautiful hands. Thank you for supporting me, and being my first reader, my sounding board and my all-around favorite guy. Even though I didn't use your idea for *Dylan O'Driscoll: Gentleman Rake*, I appreciate all of your input.

To my friends, who always understand when I say I'm writing and can't leave the house.

1

I REALLY SHOULDN'T be here. The phrase looped through Maya's brain. *I really, really shouldn't be here.* The ice cubes in her glass clinked together as she stirred her vodka-cranberry drink and took a sip. The deafening, bass-heavy music and many sweaty bodies pulsed around her as she quickly crossed the dance floor to return to the booth where her best friend and roommate, Abby, was sitting alone, waiting for her. Feeling a headache coming on, Maya frowned and pressed the heel of her hand against her forehead.

"Could you at least pretend you're having a good time?" Abby leaned in and yelled against her ear to be heard over the music. "This is the hottest club in Montreal, we both look fabulous and we're getting a ton of male attention tonight." As if to make her point, she waved to a group of men at a nearby table who were looking in their direction.

"I'm sorry," Maya yelled back. She really wanted to go home. But she also didn't want to ruin her friend's night. Abby had put a lot of effort into dragging Maya out. Earlier that evening, at home, Maya had spent far too long styling her hair into waves, although the end result was supposed to have looked as though she hadn't spent any time styling it. While constantly reloading YouTube tutorials, she had studiously worked until she achieved things called smoky eyes and contouring. It was then that Maya had decided it was all too much work, and was about to change into yoga pants and a tank top and curl up on the couch when Abby had selected her littlest black dress and strutted into Maya's room proclaiming it *the one*.

"Maya, every guy in that club is going to be drooling over you in this," Abby had assured her.

"Great," Maya had replied, without much enthusiasm. "I hope all that saliva comes out at the dry cleaners."

But she was forced to admit, thanks to Abby's instruction and help with styling, makeup and hair techniques, Maya had never looked better.

"I'm getting such a headache. And I should really get home. Finals are coming up. And we've got that early class tomorrow—" Maya grasped for any reason to not be at Swerve Nightclub on a Thursday night.

"God, you're practically agoraphobic!" Abby huffed in frustration.

"I'm not agoraphobic. I'm an introvert, and it's super trendy right now. Thank-you-very-much." *It's cute to be introverted*, she thought defensively. Words she wouldn't dare say to her friend. There were an abundance of articles and listicles online proclaiming such a thing. *It's good to have some mystery about you. And who is more mysterious than a girl who never leaves her house?*

"Either way, you're not going anywhere!" Abby pulled on Maya's wrist until she was seated at the table with her. "Don't worry about class. Dr. C. invited in some guest speaker, so it'll just be some long-winded, ancient colleague of his. They'll turn down the lights and we can nap in the back."

Maya opened her mouth, but Abby plowed over her, running her fingers through her own flawlessly styled, bleach-blond pixie haircut. "We're here to have fun. For the past few years, I've watched you lock yourself in your room, hibernate in the library and never take a minute to look up from your books. We are graduating in two weeks—" she reached out to grab Maya's hands in her own "—and I need to see you act like the beautiful, exotic, sassy young thing that you are before we part ways, become old hags and never see each other or have any fun ever again." Abby took a long pull on her beer. "We need to act young and stupid, this one last time," she pleaded. "Be irresponsible. Live a little with me."

Maya laughed. "Hey. I have fun."

Abby raised an eyebrow, clearly not convinced. "Staying home on Friday night and binge-watching *Orange Is the New Black* on Netflix isn't the type of fun that a single twenty-five-year-old woman should be having. Especially a complete knockout like yourself. When was the last time you had sex?"

Maya's mouth dropped open, shocked that her friend would even go there. "What?"

Abby smirked. "That's what I thought." She relented. "Okay, when was the last time you were even kissed?" Maya remained silent. "Your last date?"

Maya sighed. Abby was right. It had been so long since she'd been on a date, or gone to a nightclub, or even let herself focus on anything but school. But she was so close to the end. She'd spent every waking moment of the past five years working diligently toward her goal, completing her master's degree in Business Administration. For the entirety of her short adult life, it was her dream to pursue a career in hotel management, running an upscale resort hotel. Probably on a beach. Most definitely somewhere hot. She dreamed of a life in Miami, or the Bahamas, or any other exotic location in the Caribbean. She could only smile at how close she finally was to that life.

Abby continued, pressing her argument, at which she was so talented. "We're part of the hospitality industry. And in order to be successful we need to monitor trends to stay on top of our game. And at least one small part of that, my friend, includes visiting nightclubs and having fun! Trying new drinks, networking, schmoozing a little and learning to talk to people to get information about things they like and things they don't. Getting a sense of what's hot and what's not—and this place is hot, by the way. Don't you want to be at the top of your game, Maya?" Abby finished with a smile, obviously proud of herself for putting their girls' night out in terms of their studies, knowing Maya would respond favorably. Really, it was her only hope of getting her to stick around.

Maya smiled back at Abby. She loved her friend dearly, despite the fact she sometimes wanted to maim her. "You wench," she said with a laugh. Once again, Abby was right. Maya sighed and brought her glass to her lips and drank back a fortifying gulp. When the glass was empty, she slammed it down on the table. "Fine. You win. Let's have fun." Then she stopped and looked at Abby quizzically. "How do we have fun?"

"We start with me getting us more drinks." Abby stood, picking up Maya's empty glass and her own empty bottle. "That round did not last long enough."

Abby straightened her crop top and smoothed her hands down over her skinny leather pants and she made her way back to the bar.

Maya pulled out her phone to check her email, seeing nothing new, she opened her Facebook app. She flicked through the pictures that some of her friends had posted, people her age going out to clubs and having parties. They somehow managed to juggle their studies and their social lives. She scrolled lower and lower and saw more friends having drinks at pubs and eating in restaurants, hiking, playing paintball and riding on party buses. She tapped on the icon to view her own profile. There were no pictures, and at no time had she ever ridden on a party bus. Was Abby right? Had Maya let a good part of her twenties escape her without getting out there and doing wild things? *Maya, you're twenty-five. You've never gone skinny-dipping in the park or drunk a bottle of wine by the ocean.* She looked in disgust at her mostly pathetic Facebook profile and grimaced. *No more, Maya. You're going to have some fun tonight even if it kills you.*

"And it just might," she whispered to herself, as Abby walked back to the table, holding two fresh drinks for them.

"That was quick," Maya remarked, accepting her glass.

"Yeah, but I schmoozed the good-looking bartender earlier, so when he saw me walking up, he skipped everyone else at the bar to serve me." Abby smiled.

"That's awful. But nicely done." Maya proffered her glass in salute and Abby clinked it with her beer bottle. "So what are we going to do?" she asked.

Abby pursed her lips, deep in thought. Maya watched

her as she scanned the club, searching for inspiration. "How about a little truth or dare?"

"What?" Maya scoffed. "We aren't twelve anymore. I'm not going to tell you who I *like*." She giggled. It seemed that the vodka in her cranberry was working its way through her brain.

"Okay, how about dare, then?"

"Mmm, Abby, I don't know…" Maya hesitated.

"You said you wanted to have fun," Abby pleaded. "Come on, I'll do anything you dare me to do."

"Well, that's easy for you," she said, smiling broadly as she put a comforting hand on her friend's arm, "because you have no shame."

Abby laughed. "Even so." She continued scoping out the club. "Oh, I've got it."

"What?"

She pointed to the bar. Well, she was actually pointing to a gorgeous male specimen who was standing next to it, chatting with the bartender. "See that guy?"

Am I blind? How could I possibly miss a man like that? "Yeah, of course I do."

Abby pasted on her most devilish smile and directed it at Maya. "Good. Because you are going to walk up to him, wrap your arms around his neck and you're going to kiss him like you've never kissed a man before."

"I am absolutely *not* doing that," Maya insisted.

"It's a little harmless dare. What have you got to lose?"

"My pride, my dignity…" Maya trailed off. She looked at the man. It looked as though he had left work and came to the nightclub. He wore tailored pants that showed off his very nice, round behind. He had unbuttoned the top button of his shirt and had rolled up his sleeves. She watched him laugh as the bartender said something to him. *What could it hurt to walk up to him and kiss him? It's not like I'll ever see him again, a city this size...*

She thought of her sad, little, unexciting Facebook profile and Maya slammed her glass down, sloshing some of the pink liquid over the edge and onto her fingers and the table. *What the hell?* Abby was right. It had been a long time since she'd done anything other than what was expected of her. "Okay." She looked determinedly at the man. "I'm going to do it."

"Yay!" Abby raised her arms giddily in celebration as Maya walked away from the table.

JAMIE SELLERS TOOK a satisfied look around his packed club. As the owner, if there was one person to thank for the popularity of Swerve Nightclub, it was him. In fact, he owned all twelve Swerve nightclubs located throughout the country, from Vancouver to St. John's. His clubs were frequented by celebrities and professional athletes, and even some royalty graced his establishments. And quite often, his picture was posted on gossip blogs right alongside them, with headlines like "Jamie Sellers Lands a Princess", "Sellers and the Heiress" and "Nightclub Mogul Parties Hard with Hockey Team." Jamie shook his head, chuckling at the latest story linking him with the daughter of a prominent local politician.

He was young, single, rich and good-looking. That's what people saw when they looked at him. When people saw a picture of him standing next to a beautiful woman, he was automatically sleeping with her. If he'd actually slept with every woman that the so-called press had reported he did...well, he certainly wouldn't have time to be the nightclub mogul they proclaimed him to be. While it would be nice if he found himself frequently in the beds of actresses and celebutantes, it simply, sadly, was not the case.

If a picture of him holding a beer bottle or a glass of whisky surfaced? Automatically, he was portrayed as an alcoholic, a chronic drug user, a degenerate who partied too hard every night. At first, he found it easy to laugh at how inaccurate the stories were—*any press is good press, right?*—but it was starting to wear thin. The fifteen-hour days that he typically put into his work were starting to exhaust him, and the extreme workdays had gotten far more frequent and longer since his assistant quit. Typically, he found only just enough free time in a day to eat, shower, hopefully hit the gym and maybe get a few hours of sleep.

Sure. Maybe ten years ago that reputation would have been warranted. Jamie had grown up with nothing and his first taste of success had been sweet. He had admittedly overindulged in his youth, in alcohol, women, wild antics. But it was local reporter scumbag John Power who had been the catalyst for his turnaround. Power had gotten a hold of a picture of Jamie with a model enjoying a, *ahem*, private moment, and then he uncovered more and more of Jamie's bad deeds. He'd dredged up the details of Jamie's less-than-ideal childhood, with an absentee father and a drug-addict mother, a past that Jamie had guarded carefully. To say it was embarrassing was an understatement. Jamie had been cannon fodder for the reporter, who seemingly made a career of gathering information on him.

Since then, Jamie had kept it clean. He no longer overindulged. He never partied. He focused on business and it had paid off. Jamie had enjoyed an unimaginable level of success. Still, no matter how many nightclubs he opened, how much he gave to charity or how often his company showed up on lists of preferred employers, people still saw him as the millionaire, bad boy womanizer.

"Not bad for a Thursday," Jamie remarked to Trevor—one of his best friends, and definitely the best bartender he had ever met—sipping the cola Trevor had handed him.

Trevor finished pouring a pair of martinis and handed them off to a waitress. "Yeah, it must be the warm weather. Normally the end of semester makes the students hunker down, studying. But this place is clearly bumping tonight," he said, throwing an appreciative glance over the scantily clad women dancing against each other on the dance floor.

"Keep it professional, Trev," Jamie warned with a glare, before laughing. He knew that he had nothing to worry about with his friend. Trevor was a pro and would never overserve a guest, or use his position to take advantage of the young women who patronized the club. But it didn't stop him from appreciating the female beauty that was in front of him.

Jamie bit back a yawn, and Trevor regarded him carefully. "Why don't you go on home? I've got this."

"I know you do. But I've got a few things to finish up tonight. It's been crazy since Martin left." Jamie frowned at the thought of his former assistant. "I've got a couple of early morning meetings tomorrow and then I have to head to the university and give a talk with some graduate class about entrepreneurship, and entertainment, and hospitality, and yada yada yada."

"Really? That doesn't sound like something you

would normally do," Trevor said, raising an eyebrow. "Sounds like somebody is hot for teacher?"

Jamie was almost too tired to smirk at the quip. "It's nothing like that, smart guy. The professor is Dr. Carmichael."

"I see."

"So, I owe him. It's really the least I can do."

"Oh, of course." Trevor nodded. "Dr. C. And you're doing this at the expense of any sleep you might get tonight?"

"I'll sleep when I'm dead." Jamie took another sip of his drink and turned to survey his nightclub.

A packed club was always good news for Jamie, and there had been plenty of that as of late. All of his nightclubs were outperforming expectations on a nightly basis. But his brain was always working, knowing that he had to keep the guest experience fresh in each of his clubs to keep people coming back. Every time he looked around, he saw areas for improvement. Ways to make the continuous lineup to the front door more efficient, an enhanced VIP experience, flair bartenders and entertainers, A-list DJs and performers, the list was always growing.

It was while he was surveying his domain, rolling through his mental to-do list, that he noticed a stunning woman walk toward him. She wasn't just stunning; she was actually the most beautiful woman he had ever seen. Her long hair cascaded in loose waves over her shoulders, and a little black dress highlighted legs that seemed to go on forever. She was looking straight at him, making a beeline for where he was standing at the bar. He sighed quietly. She obviously knew who he was. She wanted to cozy up to the single, rich owner of Swerve. Even though he was a fan of her beauty, he was exhausted and he didn't have time for the attention of groupies tonight, no matter how gorgeous.

When she was close enough to him, he extended his hand to her and put on his most cordial smile. "Hi, can I help—"

His words were stopped in his throat when her arms wrapped around his neck and pulled him forward until his lips found hers. His eyes widened as she kissed him. But they soon closed when he felt her tongue stroke his bottom lip. He stifled a moan and opened his mouth, to let himself be taken over by the feeling of this mysterious women in his arms.

Jamie couldn't remember ever being kissed so fiercely by a woman. Everything else seemed to disappear. There was no music, no flashing lights, no crowd of thirsty patrons lined up at the bar, no Trevor, who was surely staring at them, agog.

It was when his hands found her hips, the spell broke and the sounds and lights of the club and all of the people around them came rushing back. She broke away from him. Still standing just inches apart, he saw the flush that stained her face and felt her breath on his chin. He got a good look at her and the thing that stood out most was the frightened, guilty look in those amazingly dark, almond-shaped eyes. She was a second from hightailing it away from him, out of his life, and he knew it. He wanted to ask her name, maybe buy her a drink, anything to make her stay.

After a beat, she shook out of her trance, mumbled an "I'm so sorry," and did exactly what he thought she would. She turned on her heel and walked away, almost running, disappearing in the crowd of bodies on the dance floor.

Jamie was rendered speechless for a moment, before he turned to Trevor, bewildered and out of breath. "Do you know who she was?"

Trevor laughed heartily. "I have no idea. You didn't know her? It definitely seemed as if you two were familiar. Wait a minute!" Trevor snapped his fingers in a moment of inspiration and turned to the computer behind the bar and consulted the names of the customers who had started drink tabs. "Maya Connor is her name. She's here with a friend, she's drinking vodka-cran and the friend is a light-beer girl."

Jamie ran a hand through his dark hair and checked his watch. "I've got to head back upstairs." He turned to go, but stopped and faced Trevor again. "Take care of their tab, will you? Make sure they get whatever they want."

"Will do, boss," Trevor replied with a smirk.

WHEN MAYA RETURNED to Abby, it seemed that her friend had made a friend of her own. Maya watched Abby as she talked to a gentleman who had taken up residence at their booth. Maya scooted in on the far side and looked at the stranger.

"Beat it, bud." She hooked a thumb over her shoulder and scowled. When he left with a confused shrug, she buried her face in her hands. "Oh, my God! I can't believe I kissed him!" Realizing that her own glass was empty, she reached across the table and snatched Abby's beer bottle from her hands.

"Hey!" Abby yelled, attempting to take back her drink. Maya assumed that she was more upset about her stolen drink than she was about the newly vacated seat next to her.

"I can't believe you dared me to do that." Maya looked back at the bar and saw that the man she had kissed was gone, but the bartender was still there. She was suddenly parched, and she certainly couldn't go back up there. She didn't think she could even face him again. How was she supposed to get another drink? Or even pay her tab when they were ready to leave? She'd thought of none of those things when she had made the stupidest, most impulsive decision of her life in kissing the stranger at the bar. "Oh, God, I need another drink."

"So get your own drink." Abby snatched back her bottle. "I cannot believe you actually kissed him! I'm superimpressed."

Maya measured the distance between herself and the bar and caught the eye of the bartender, who was watching her with curiosity. "I can't go back up there. He was talking to the bartender like they were friends or something. I just can't do it."

Abby pushed herself up from the table. "Fine, I'll get you something. Vodka? Or do you want something a little crazier in celebration of your turn as a woman who kisses strange men in a bar?"

Maya brought her forehead to the table. "Vodka's fine," she muttered.

With Abby gone, Maya had a chance to think about what she had done. What if the man wasn't single? She hadn't seen a wedding ring, but that didn't mean anything. He could have taken it off—*which would make him the scummiest guy in the world*—or maybe he had a girlfriend. *Does that make me a home wrecker? Not if I haven't actually wrecked his home.* And she wasn't going to do that. She had no intention of actually seeing him again.

And, holy shit, she had basically assaulted him! Maya began to panic as the thought overtook her. If a man had walked up to her and just kissed her, forcing his tongue in her own mouth, she would be outraged! He would definitely be rinsing her pepper spray from his eyes and icing his groin all night. *How dare you, Maya?* If she ever saw him again, she would definitely have to apologize, grovel even. She felt awful. This would be the absolute last time she "lived a little." She didn't understand how Abby could do whatever she wanted without worrying about the consequences of her actions. But it certainly wasn't how Maya chose to live her life. Not by a long shot.

She was almost shaking with panic when Abby came back to the table with their drinks and pushed the pink one toward her. "The cute bartender Trevor poured you a double. He figured you needed it."

"Oh, my," she sighed. She took a drink and grimaced at the taste of the extra alcohol. She drank again, and this time the beverage slid down her throat more easily. She wasn't a big drinker, but with the strength of the drink, plus the two or three she'd had earlier, she started to feel her uneasiness and panic slip away. A warm sensation rose from her belly and she felt herself relax a little.

"So," Abby said, taking a sip of her beer. "Tell me about the kiss."

The kiss. Maya could still feel his lips on hers, and the coarse stubble of the five o'clock shadow that covered that strong, broad jaw grazing roughly against the soft skin of her face. She could smell his cologne, a blend of citrus, sandalwood, innate maleness. And she heard his groan, which had vibrated through her when his lips parted and his tongue found hers. Maya recalled the sense of loss she had felt when she'd pulled away. Kissing him was wrong, but that didn't stop her from wanting to feel the dark, handsome stranger all over her body.

And Abby wanted her to tell her about the kiss? How could she put it into words? Were there any words to describe the feeling of being pressed against him? She struggled to find them, to come up with anything that would even come close to relating the experience to another person.

"It was good," she said simply, knowing that *good* didn't even come remotely close to describing the kiss.

"'It was good,'" Abby repeated, clearly unconvinced. "Just 'good'?"

"It was really, very good," she said with a shrug.

Abby laughed. "The way you looked when you came back to this table told me that it was more than just 'really, very good.'"

Maya flushed, suddenly warm. From the temperature of the club? The alcohol? Her reaction to the man? "What does it matter?" Maya finished her drink in one long swallow, dismissing it. "He's a great kisser. But in this city? It's not like I'm going to see him again."

Abby smirked, pursing her cherry-red lips. "Montreal might be the second largest city in the country, but I think it's smaller than you think. You just might encounter him again."

Maya leaned back in the booth, the back of her head resting on the plush leather upholstery. She inhaled deeply. Yeah, the alcohol was definitely pumping through her veins. She quickly put the gorgeous man at the bar out of her mind. She was now ready to have fun.

When a song she loved drove through the speakers of the club's sound system, she stood quickly. A little too quickly, as evidenced by her slight wobble. She grabbed Abby's hand.

"Come on, we're dancing!"

Abby's mouth dropped in surprise and she squealed with glee. "It's about time, Maya. I love the new you."

At that moment Maya did, as well. The music pumped, as did her body to the beat. She focused on nothing else but how she felt at that moment. She dismissed all thoughts of her upcoming final exams and her 9 a.m. class, and she allowed Abby to pull her into the center of the dance floor. But neither her mind nor her body could forget the handsome stranger. In an attempt to shake his image from her mind and the feel of his lips burning on her own, she danced harder. But it was no use; he wouldn't leave her. Perhaps instead of just kissing him, she should have talked to him, asked him his name, gotten his number.

Maya stopped dancing, however, when some movement caught her eye. It was him, and he was standing on a staircase which overlooked the dance floor. He stood with his arms crossed over his chest. And she was transfixed when he raised his hand to scrub along the rough bristles of his jaw, before dragging it through his dark hair.

It would have been her chance—to go up and talk to him. If only she had time to cross through the packed dance floor to get to him. She felt a sharp pang of remorse when he turned and walked up the dark staircase, forever relegating himself to her memory as the *handsome stranger*. She shook her head at the events of the evening. *It was fun, but it was definitely over.*

2

THE NEXT MORNING Maya awoke with the worst hangover of her life—not that she had many in her life to compare it to—but this was definitely the worst! She groaned at the buzzing alarm on her cell phone and, with her eyes tightly shut, felt around her night table for it. When she couldn't manage to turn it off with her eyes still closed, she threw it into the pile of dirty clothes in the corner of her room. But much to her chagrin, doing so did nothing to silence the dreadful racket, and she pulled her comforter over her head.

Once Maya managed to roll out of her bed, she pulled on a tank top and a pair of shorts. She padded barefoot to the kitchen, where she found Abby sitting at the narrow breakfast bar, with her head on the table—thankfully she had managed to make some coffee.

"Can we just skip class today?" Abby pleaded, obviously not faring any better than Maya. "Also, can we just skip today, in general? And don't answer too loudly. Please."

Maya poured herself a cup of coffee and sighed. "I wish we could do both of those things, but you know

Carmichael is gonna test us somehow on the guest lecturer."

"Why is he so evil?" Abby whined.

"Because he's tenured." Maya laughed quietly. "Also he's a very sweet old man and not at all evil, and you know it. And he didn't make us stay out last night until 3 a.m." She closed her eyes and groaned. God, 3 a.m. It had been years since Maya had even thought about staying up that late. She brought the mug to her lips, holding back a slight wave of nausea as she sipped her black coffee.

"Don't remind me," Abby groaned. "Oh, man, we were out so late. I don't even want to know how much I owe you for all those drinks."

Maya opened her mouth, but the words stopped as a thought struck her. "Huh. Actually, I just remembered something. I didn't pay anything for them. When I went to settle my tab, the bartender told me it was taken care of."

"Really? Taken care of?" Abby raised her head. "What does that mean?"

"I don't know who, but someone paid for our drinks. I didn't think about it too much because I was so drunk." She pursed her lips in question. "Who would do that?"

"I have no idea," Abby replied, raising her eyes to meet Maya's. "Unless it was that man you sucked face with." She grinned. "Wait. That wasn't grammatically correct, was it? Uh, how about 'the man with whom you sucked face'?"

Maya's mouth dropped. "What? No. That's not possible. Why would he do that? Why would he pay for all of those drinks? It couldn't have been cheap."

"Well, I don't know. Perhaps it has something to do

with the gorgeous, exotic creature who walked up to him and shoved her tongue down his throat," Abby surmised. "Maybe he thought you would find him again, to properly thank him for taking care of your tab. You said he seemed friendly with the bartender."

Maya rolled her eyes, grimacing at the resulting headache. She would have to remind herself not to move her eyes for the rest of the day. "He thought I would *repay* him? That's just gross." She took a gulp of coffee, finished it and placed her empty mug in the sink. "And please, don't remind me about that whole kissing-a-stranger thing," Maya pleaded, glancing at the time. "And, to make this morning even better, we're going to be late for class. I call first shower."

CLASS HAD ALREADY started when Maya and Abby arrived, sunglasses on and heads pounding. They opened the closed door as inconspicuously as they could, to avoid attracting too much attention. They drew the eyes of the twenty-six other students in the class as well as Dr. Carmichael, who cast a disapproving glance in their direction.

They muttered their apologies, and Maya scanned the room. Abby's plan to nap in the back was thwarted because the back rows of the small lecture hall were already occupied, and they were forced to sit at the very center of the front row.

They took their seats and Dr. Carmichael resumed his introduction of the guest lecturer. "Now that you're all here," he said, glancing at Maya and Abby. "Ladies and gentlemen, I know that your time here is drawing to a close and you're all busy studying for finals, but today I invited someone to come in and talk to you, perhaps to inspire you on your paths in business and in the hospitality industry. The remarkable young man you are about to meet has done so much since he was my student, including becoming one of the most successful businessmen in his industry as a, how do the papers put it, nightclub mogul?" The professor laughed to himself. "Students, please welcome the owner of Swerve nightclubs, Jamie Sellers."

The professor got Maya's attention at his mention of Swerve Nightclub, and her eyes sharpened. But her mouth completely dropped when she actually got a good look at the man walking into her classroom. Jamie Sellers. The man she had kissed the night before. The owner of the damn club. The man who had paid for their many, many drinks and, if it was possible, looked even more gorgeous than he had the night before. Maya cast a quick look at Abby, whose eyes were as wide in shock as Maya's, and she silently hyperventilated in her seat. In an act of desperation, she took a look under her desk. *Is there enough room to crawl under there and die?*

Maya watched Jamie's acute eyes survey the class until they settled on her, sitting front-row center. Their eyes connected and she nearly trembled under his scrutiny. How could she be expected to sit still for fifty minutes with him in front of her? Mortification and sudden desire made her flush and she could feel her temperature rise.

Their eyes held for a beat too long, and Maya held her breath. She was relieved when his gaze roamed elsewhere. He cleared his throat. "Hey, guys. I don't normally do things like this, but when Dr. Carmichael asked me to come in, how could I say no?" He cast an affectionate glance toward the professor. "Because I don't believe that I would be the person I am today if not for him and his intervention.

"You see, I wasn't always a 'nightclub mogul.'" Jamie smiled and made air quotes around the phrase with his fingers. "I was a punk kid, my parents were never around and I just barely graduated from high school. I got into trouble quite frequently. But I met Dr. Carmichael one night while I was working as a busboy." Jamie briefly described his history with Dr. Carmichael, and Maya admired how far Jamie had come in such a short amount of time. "He showed me that if you have a passion for something, no matter what's standing in your way, you should go for it, and that doesn't just apply in business, but in everyday life, as well."

Jamie spoke with an enthusiasm to which Maya could relate, and she smiled, seeing a lot of herself in the man before her. She admired him already. As he told them the story of shedding the weight of a troubled upbringing and his transformation to successful business-owner, she held on to his every word.

"I wasn't going to make a splash just washing glasses for a decade." He laughed, as did many of the people in her class. "Although, as the boss, I fully appreciate each and every employee under me, from the busboys and waitresses to my club managers and executives. It is a team environment, and you should never forget that it is the people that matter most. If your people are happy, they'll be motivated and make your customers happy. If you've got happy workers and happy customers, the profit won't be far behind."

Everything Jamie was saying made perfect sense to Maya, but it was when he looked at her that it seemed she could barely think straight. When his eyes connected

with hers, she couldn't hear what was going on around
her or what he or anyone else in the class was saying.
She could hear nothing but the sound of her heart beat-
ing in her ears. When his gaze connected with hers, she
could only manage to fidget with her fingers, her pen.
She straightened some papers on her desk, and then she
straightened them again. Anything so she wouldn't have
to look back at the man in front of her. The man who
seemingly made her cheeks flush and her skin tingle
with a single stare.

AFTER ONE OF the most uncomfortable hours of his life,
Jamie said goodbye to the class and wished them luck
in their future careers. He shook Dr. Carmichael's hand
and quickly left the classroom. He stopped in the hallway
outside to pull out his phone to see how many calls, texts
and emails he had missed. There were many of each. He
sighed. Once again, he thought of the empty assistant's
desk in the corner of his office and remembered that he
had to get on with hiring someone new. Martin wasn't
coming back, no matter what price Jamie offered him.

Jamie put his phone to his ear, when he felt the soft
touch of a hand on his arm. He turned and saw her. Maya
Connor. The woman from the bar last night. The woman
who had been sitting front and center during his talk.
How many times was he forced to tear his gaze from
her, only to have it roam, out of his control, back in her
direction. How many times had he tripped over his own
tongue when he thought of her arms around him and her
body pressed against his? More than once the blood that
fueled his brain, his speech and any logical thought he'd
formed surged south. Luckily, he'd worn dark pants, so
his innermost thoughts and desires remained secret to

the class. But the fact that he couldn't seem to control his hormones, as if he were a horny teenager, bothered him right in the control-freak tendencies.

Last night he'd watched her from the staircase leading up to his office, and he had to hold himself back from going to her. He had spent the rest of the night watching Maya from his office through the window that let him see what was happening in his club. No matter where she was in the crowd, he had always seemed to be able to find her. Like a siren in the fog, she drew him in whether he liked it or not. On the dance floor, she'd moved effortlessly to the beat of the music. He had pondered arranging a VIP table for them, but he remembered the frightened look in her eyes after she'd kissed him, and he thought better of it. He wouldn't want to scare her off, and he certainly wanted to see her back in his club again.

Jamie knew that he had to be careful. Thankfully, he hadn't seen any pictures or videos posted of their kiss. He'd spent the morning scouring the worst of the online tabloids, especially *Montreal Secrets*, run by John Power, which had been decidedly poor in their treatment of him since he'd opened his first club.

In this case, he'd gotten lucky. He couldn't afford any bad press as he was about to embark on one of the most daunting projects of his life, and he certainly didn't have time to be in a relationship, or even just casually see anyone. Every bit of focus had to be put toward his work.

"Listen, Mr. Sellers," Maya said, interrupting his thoughts. She averted her eyes and was clearly embarrassed. He enjoyed the way her brow creased and the way she brought her bottom lip between her teeth.

Jamie was watching her mouth, wishing that his lips, teeth and tongue were there, joined with hers. So he didn't realize that she was still speaking and he had to force his eyes back to hers. The beautiful, dark, almond eyes he recalled from the previous night. He was lost.

"I'm really sorry about last night," she stammered. "I shouldn't have kissed you. It was inappropriate, and it was—"

"It's okay," he said, assuring her with a smile.

"It's really not," she insisted. "It's just that my friend Abby dared me to do something reckless, and I'd had a bit too much to drink. Oh, and can I assume you paid for our drinks?" He nodded. "It was sweet, but really not necessary. Here, let me pay you back." She reached into her purse and pulled out her wallet. "How much do I owe you? I made sure to tip the bartender. I hope it was enough for how much the bill must have been—"

He put a hand on hers, stilling her. "Don't." He forced himself to ignore the sizzle he felt when his fingers touched hers. "Keep your money. It's not a big deal. It was only a couple of drinks."

She laughed. The sound pulsed pleasantly through him. "I think it was more than a couple, if how I felt this morning was any indication. And for your information, just so we're clear, that's not why I kissed you. This isn't some scam I have to get free drinks. I didn't even know who you were. I just thought you were some sexy guy at the bar—" She stopped suddenly, and her eyes widened, the flush returning to her cheeks. She laughed once more, shakily, bringing her palm to her forehead. "I'm rambling again, aren't I? I do that when I'm nervous. I just can't stop talking sometimes. It's this thing I do." She was speaking so quickly that Jamie could barely keep up. She gesticulated wildly. "I say something embarrassing, and then I keep talking to try and talk my way out of it. And I just can't stop myself. I go on and on and on and on. And I can't stop." She paused. "I should just stop talking, shouldn't I?"

It was Jamie's turn to laugh. This woman was not only gorgeous, but she was also absolutely delightful to be around. "I really wish you wouldn't." He opened his mouth to continue when he heard a familiar voice over his shoulder.

"Jamie, Maya," Dr. Carmichael said, placing an arm over each of their shoulders. "I'm glad you had a chance to get acquainted." He smiled indulgently at them both. "Jamie, Maya is one of the finest students I've ever had the pleasure of teaching."

Jamie looked at her, wonder raising his eyebrows. He knew that Dr. C.'s compliments were not easy to come by. He'd had to work long and hard before he had earned any of his own. He knew Maya must be something special to have deserved such commendation. "Is that right? That's certainly high praise, indeed." He nodded appreciatively. "Any plans for after graduation?"

She exhaled slightly and allowed the rigidity in her posture to relax slightly. The shift was subtle, but he noticed. Clearly, she was a woman who was most at ease with her work.

"I've got nothing concrete lined up yet, but I'm interested in hotel management," she told him, her voice giving away the fact that she had definitely memorized the answer and used it often. "I've got a career path that I'd like to follow to make that happen."

"That's great. It's important to stay focused on your goals." Jamie's phone started ringing in his left hand, and he held out his right to Maya. "Maya, it was a pleasure meeting you *today*," he added for emphasis, before turning to his mentor. "Dr. C., I'll be in touch. Let's have dinner some night when I'm not quite so bogged down with work."

The professor smiled. "Well, son, unless you've changed your ways recently, I don't know when that will be."

Jamie regretted not having time to catch up with his mentor. A man who had done so much for him and his career. "Thanks for having me."

"Thanks for coming in, Jamie." The man shook his hand and gave him a pat on the shoulder before releasing him, his eyes twinkling with obvious pride. "Look after yourself. But make sure you focus on what's really important in life."

Jamie looked quizzically at the professor before putting his phone to his ear, turning his back on the old man and the single most beautiful woman he had ever met. He had important business to conduct with the contractor on the other end, but it didn't stop him from thinking about the woman who had come into his life, catching him off guard for the second time in just under twelve hours. He pushed all thoughts of Maya out of his mind. He had work to do, and he certainly didn't have time for indulging fantasies of gorgeous graduate students.

"Scott, good to hear from you," he said into the phone, pushing through the doors to the warm spring air.

3

LATER THAT NIGHT, Jamie still sat at his desk. Almost everyone else had gone home for the day, but Jamie remained. He needed to review some construction estimates and vendor contracts in order to begin construction on the new hotel he planned to build. This was the next step in his company's future—upscale boutique hotels boasting the Sellers and Swerve name. Jamie shuffled through the stacks of papers and file folders on his desk. *How did I get so unorganized?*

Out of habit he looked over at the empty desk in the corner of the room that Martin once occupied. He sighed, lamenting his assistant's absence and realized more every day how much he had come to depend on having someone else to help him shoulder the considerable workload. He thumbed through another stack of contracts, looking for a contractor's quote that he needed for his newest acquisition—a small building he had bought in foreclosure near the downtown Swerve. He threw down the papers with a frustrated sigh and picked up his phone. Moving his fingers quickly, he typed out a message to his secretary, Mary, asking her to place an ad for a new assistant as soon as possible.

Jamie didn't know what he would do without Mary. Like Trevor, she had been with him since the beginning, and she was integral in making sure the day-to-day operations ran smoothly.

He rubbed his eyes and let his thoughts roam once again to Maya Connor. With a smile, he recalled their encounters in the past twenty-four hours. First, she had kissed him and then she was sitting front-row center in Dr. C.'s class for his lecture, and then she approached him afterward, apologizing and offering to repay him in the most adorable way possible. Dr. Carmichael had called her his best student, and she must be to have earned his adoration. She would be finishing school in a couple of weeks, no actual job lined up just yet. Perhaps. Just perhaps...

Before he could stop himself, tell himself that it was a bad idea, Jamie picked up the phone and dialed a familiar number.

CURLED UP ON the couch with a wool blanket over her legs, Maya settled in after she reached for her bowl of popcorn. She didn't care what Abby thought. Curling up on the couch and binge-watching Netflix was fun. *All the fun I need, in fact.* She queued up the next episode of *Orange Is the New Black* and sat back, letting the plush couch cuddle her in a way that no man would ever know how.

Jamie Sellers might know how, she conceded. The man looked as wicked as sin, and those strong arms she'd felt wrap around her, and those delicious lips she'd touched with her own, would certainly know how to hold and caress all of the most sensitive parts of her body.

Realizing that she had been lost in thoughts of Jamie Sellers and not paying attention to the beginning of the episode, she stopped to rewind it when her phone rang. She picked it up to look at the screen and frowned when she didn't recognize the number as she brought it to her ear. "Hello?" she mumbled through a mouthful of popcorn.

"Is this Maya Connor?" a masculine voice that she knew, but couldn't place, rumbled into her ear and throughout her body.

"Um, yes." Try as she might, she couldn't place the familiar voice.

"Hi, this is Jamie Sellers."

What? She choked slightly as she swallowed her popcorn with her now-dry throat. "Oh, hello."

"Well, this might seem like it's coming out of nowhere." Now it was Jamie's turn to hesitate. He cleared his throat. "And I'm sorry to bother you at home. I got your number from Dr. Carmichael. But I recall you saying you didn't yet have a job lined up after graduation."

"Yes, that's right." She furrowed her brow and pulled her lip between her teeth. *What is this? Why is he calling?*

"Well, I was wondering if you would consider coming to work for me."

What? "I'm sorry?"

"My assistant just quit, and I'm getting buried with more work than I can manage with each passing day. And I know it's not a post-graduate-level job and you're probably overqualified for it, but I'm being straightforward, working for me would provide you with a stepping-stone in your career path. I could give you some great work experience and introduce you to some important people."

He was right. While she hadn't counted on doing the work of an assistant after she graduated, working for Jamie Sellers would be a golden opportunity she couldn't turn down. Her thoughts turned to the stack of job ads that she had printed, waiting for her on her desk. And then she pictured the faces of the twenty-seven other people in her graduating class, all of whom would be vying for the same jobs in a matter of weeks. Maya could guarantee that none of them currently had Jamie Sellers on the phone offering them a position.

"So how about it?"

"I'm still in school." She closed her eyes, hoping he wouldn't change his mind and hire someone who was actually available right away. "I still have finals."

"That's fine. I understand that. We can work around your class and exam schedule until you finish up. I'm just afraid that if I wait much longer, I'll be buried alive in stacks of paper," he chuckled, before pausing. "So, you'll do it?"

Maya remained silent.

"Ms. Connor?"

She opened her mouth to speak, but no words came out. Shock had her sitting up straight, eyes wide. So, she took a deep breath, confident that her life was about to change. "I'll do it, Mr. Sellers. Thank you for the opportunity."

Jamie breathed a sigh. Was he holding his breath? "That's great, you won't regret it. Why don't you call me back tomorrow morning, anytime between 9:00

and 12:00 would be great. You can talk to my secretary, Mary. She'll be expecting your call and she'll get your information and find a convenient time for you to come in for a face-to-face."

A FEW DAYS LATER, Maya sat in the waiting area of Jamie's office. She drummed her nails on her thigh and thought about how quickly her life was changing. In just a few days she would finally be finished with her degree. After years of hard work just to put some letters after her name, being so close to the end felt incredible. Maya Connor, *MBA*. To top it all off, she would be skipping the grueling cycle of résumé writing and job interviews to start her career right out of the gate as Jamie Sellers's assistant.

Sitting outside Jamie's office, about to start her career, was exciting. She had been surprised when she was told to meet him at Swerve Nightclub. The evening that she'd kissed him, she had caught a final glimpse of him, as he climbed the stairs, but she'd had no idea that those stairs led to the swanky, upscale, trendy offices and waiting room that the space above the club boasted. The large panels of glass, most likely double-sided and definitely soundproofed, looked down on the club, and she could see it all from a different perspective. From the vantage point of her chair in Jamie's waiting room, she was brought back to the night she and Abby had been here. She could see the booth where she and Abby had sat and the dance floor where they had gyrated and swayed the night away. She saw the bar where she had kissed Jamie. She flushed slightly at the memory. She wondered whether or not he looked out those windows at her after he disappeared up the stairs. *Of course not*, she scolded herself. *Don't be ridiculous, Maya.*

She covertly sneaked glances at Mary, the somewhat older, but still quite beautiful, receptionist behind the desk. She was perfectly coifed, styled and polished within an inch of her life. Of course she was. Jamie Sellers's office gatekeeper could only be the pinnacle of style and grace.

She thought about Jamie's reputation. It's not like she had Googled him, but—okay, she'd Googled him. A quick search had revealed many news stories. Well, mostly postings on *Montreal Secrets*, in which he was reputed to have bedded all sorts of famous, glamorous and beautiful women.

Maya looked down and took in her own suit. A gray jacket and slim pants and a white blouse paired with some killer dark red heels which normally made her feel like a million bucks. She thought the ensemble was stylish and had always felt comfortable in it. However, next to Mary she felt bland and boring. She sighed quietly and consulted her watch, while her left leg twitched up and down—a nervous tic she had been scolded about since childhood.

Maya was nervous. She knew that she was overqualified for the job, but a small part of her thought that maybe, just maybe, she had been hired because she kissed him. Had her parents been right? Had he hired her because he thought she would be easy access for a little afternoon delight in the office? *I mean, he probably thinks I'm some easy girl who wouldn't think twice about lifting her skirt for her boss.* Her nerves somehow turned to anger. *How dare he? Well, I'm here to work, and if he's just looking for some office sidepiece to fill his needs, if that's what he thinks I'll be, he's wrong. I'll show him just how hard I can work as his assistant.*

"Jamie's running a little late this morning," Mary told her, interrupting her thoughts. "He shouldn't be much longer."

"Thank you," she responded with a small smile, grateful for the break from her thoughts.

"Can I get you anything? Some espresso or sparkling water?"

"No, thank you. I'm fine."

Something buzzed on Mary's desk. She touched a button on her headset. "Certainly, Jamie. She'll be right in." She turned to Maya. "You can go in now."

Maya stood and brushed imaginary lint from her pants and jacket. "Thank you." She pushed through the heavy door. And with her heart pounding against the inside of her chest, she walked slowly into the large office. She took in her surroundings and she was astounded by what she saw—a seating area with a sleek leather couch and armchair, a wet bar with a small selection of premium alcoholic beverages and a kitchenette with an espresso machine. One large window showed the city skyline for miles.

"Oh, wow, what a view," she spoke softly, to herself.

He was seated at his desk, his face obscured as he looked down at some documents. His dark hair was shiny from the sunlight that was pouring in. He was so engrossed in his work that he didn't even register her appearance in his office until she was standing in front of the desk. His head rose and she was hit with that face once again, making her gasp a little. His light blue eyes, high cheekbones, straight nose and that strong square jaw which seemed to be perpetually covered with a five o'clock shadow, even at ten in the morning, all combined to send her uncontrollable hormones into a tizzy.

"Ms. Connor," he said with a smile before standing to shake her hand. "Thanks for accepting my offer and for coming in today."

"Thank you so much for the opportunity."

He smiled again, his white teeth glistened. "Please sit down. I'll just go through the details of the job and expectations, and then you can head over to HR to get settled away with your compensation and other personnel details."

Maya relaxed when he started talking about the job. Of course, he would be professional. He didn't hire her to be his personal bedmate. He was a businessman, after all. He passed over documents and folders and explained what each one was. She nodded, attempting to keep it all straight in her head.

"If it feels like too much right now, you'll get it in time."

"I'll be fine. Thanks," she told him, balancing the files in her arms. "I do better when there's a heavy workload, or a tight deadline."

"Not a bad quality in someone working for me," he said. "We've got quite a few balls in the air right now."

"Well, I can't wait to start," she said, smiling over the reams and reams of paper that she held in her arms.

When it seemed as if he was done discussing the workload, he hesitated. He breathed deeply and sat on the corner of his desk, closest to her, and his voice got lower. "And, Maya, just so we're clear, I hired you because of the recommendation that came from Dr. Carmichael and your desire to work in hotel management. It didn't have anything to do with us kissing." He averted his gaze, as if he were nervous. Did she make him nervous? "But, let me be firm. That's not the type of organization I run here. I feel that relationships between coworkers can only lead to disaster. And nothing like that can ever happen between us again."

Maya breathed a sigh of relief. After hearing him lay out his position on their kiss, she was certain that he hired her for her professional attributes. She could do this. She could do this if they promised to keep it professional. She nodded. "It absolutely will not happen again. I wish I could take that kiss back. I really do. Thank you for the opportunity, Jamie. You won't regret it."

"I know I won't," he said, smiling at her.

HE ALREADY REGRETTED IT.

After he had sent her off to the human resources department, Jamie sighed and rubbed his hands through his dark hair. *What was I thinking hiring her?* The short time she had been in his office, he found it impossible to think of anything but how her black hair shimmered, the smell of her perfume, her sharp eyes, her smile. How could he be expected to get any work done with her sitting in his office, day in and day out?

Since the night that she'd kissed him, she was all he had been able to think about. All he wanted to do was kiss her again. To feel her hair in his hands. To rip that amazing-looking suit from her body and to feel her soft skin against his own. He groaned in frustration. *Well, she's here now. You've got to make it work somehow, Sellers.*

Steeling himself, he made a decision and pounded his fist on his desk. *I'll just do my work. Stay busy. Ignore her. That's the only way this is going to work, and we've got to keep this professional.* It wouldn't be hard to do. He regarded the stacks of paper in front of him and the phone messages that Mary had just given him. He puffed his cheeks and quickly blew out the air that he had been holding in his lungs. *All right now. Pull it together.*

Jamie's attention was drawn to the door when he heard a hesitant knock. He smiled, knowing he didn't have any appointments lined up at the moment. So it must have been Maya, returning from the human resources department. He pictured her on the other side, biting her lip, not wanting to enter without permission, but needing to enter and not knowing what to do. He pushed himself away from his desk and walked to the door. He pulled it open and his suspicions were confirmed when he saw Maya standing there, holding yet another folder that the human resources department had given her.

"Hi," she said quietly. "I didn't want to disturb you. Mary is at lunch and I didn't want to barge in."

He chuckled and moved aside so she could enter. "Maya, this is your office, as well." He ushered her in. "I hope it works for you. I like to keep my right-hand man, uh, w-woman," he stammered, "close by. But don't feel the need to knock, just come on in. If there's something going on for which I need privacy, I'll just use the conference room down the hall."

Maya nodded. "Sounds good." She walked to her own desk to address her own stack of files. Jamie noted how much brighter she made his office. It was nice having another person around in the large room again. She looked up at him and smiled brightly. "So, where should I start?"

Jamie found himself staring. He shook his head to clear the fogginess she made him feel. He dealt with the unwelcome distraction the only way he knew how, by focusing on business. "I need you to go over the contractors' quotes for work on the premier Swerve Hotel opening here in the city."

"Sounds good," she said pleasantly, though her eyes narrowed at his newly curt tone. She shrugged and located the particular folder she needed and opened it, starting her own work.

MAYA SAT QUIETLY at her own desk all afternoon. She could feel the tension rolling from his side of the office. At first, she wondered if it had something to do with her. Had she done something to displease him? She racked her brain thinking of everything that she had done or said. He never looked up from his desk, unless to ask her a specific question about her work or to answer one of hers. He barely acknowledged her existence. At first, his dismissal of her played on her mind. She thought that they were building a friendly relationship, with the easy conversation that they had shared earlier. But his new treatment of her shook her confidence.

It was when she watched him drag his hands through his dark hair, for probably the hundredth time that afternoon, she frowned. *Why are you so freaking sensitive?* She scolded herself. *This isn't about you. This guy obviously has a lot going on right now, and he doesn't have time to play nice with you, chatting all day. He hired you to do a job. So do it, Maya.*

Her eyes still on him, she watched him tent his long fingers in front of his face, obviously deep in thought. He grabbed a pen and scribbled furiously on a pad of yellow legal paper in front of him, apparently caught by a moment of inspiration.

Watching him at work, she smiled. Jamie Sellers was an impossibly good-looking man. Once again she was brought back to the night when, at the nightclub below them, she had kissed him in one of the most impulsive moments of her life. Her lips tingled and desire flushed throughout her body. Every time she thought about that kiss she had a similar reaction. But if she hoped to concentrate on anything at all this afternoon she needed to stop. Shaking herself free of the thoughts, she sighed.

Her sigh was a little too loud, as it caught Jamie's attention. He gazed over at her. His steel-blue eyes seemingly looking into her. "Everything okay?"

Caught off guard, she stammered a little. "Uh, yeah, sorry. I think I just need a cup of coffee." She recovered quickly, gesturing to the espresso machine in the kitchenette.

"Help yourself," he said, looking back down at his paperwork. "Do you know how to use one of those?"

"Yeah, my parents have one just like it." She stood. "Do you want anything?"

"Just so we're clear, your job isn't to get me coffee. I can get my own coffee," he told her, brow furrowed. "But, yeah sure, if you don't mind." He smiled. "A double espresso, no sugar or anything would be great. Thank you."

BY THE EVENING, Jamie found himself seated at the bar of the club downstairs. He watched Trevor dry the glasses he had just pulled from the washer with a microfiber cloth. Jamie smiled at the attention to detail. Neither man could abide serving glasses that had dried water spots on them.

"You all right, man?" Trevor asked him while he worked.

Jamie shoved his hand through his hair. "Yeah, I'm fine. I'm just tired."

"How's the new assistant working out?" he asked with a smirk.

Jamie regarded Trevor carefully. He obviously knew that he had hired Maya. "She's working out just fine," he answered with a curt nod.

"Can I get you a Coke?"

Jamie shook his head. "Not today. I will have a finger of the Aberfeldy 21, though. Neat."

Raising a questioning eyebrow, Trevor reached for one of their finest scotches. "Sure, friend." He reached for the bottle at the top of the display and carefully poured out a serving. "That's a strange order for you. You don't normally drink at all, let alone here. What's up?"

"Why does anything need to be up?" he demanded.

"Jamie, you're a creature of habit, some might think you're bordering on workaholic. So, what exactly is going on here?" He leaned on the bar to come face-to-face with Jamie. "Does it have anything to do with the beautiful new assistant you hired? I heard her name is Maya Connor. Funny, that happens to be the name of the woman who kissed you right here at the bar not long ago, is it not?"

Jamie threw back the scotch and swallowed it in one gulp. Normally, he would have enjoyed sipping such a decadent spirit, but right then he needed the fortification. "Yeah," he sighed, the scotch burning a pleasant trail down his throat and into his stomach. "Even though you already seem to know, it is her."

He proceeded to tell Trevor about their encounter in Dr. Carmichael's class and him offering her the job. "And for the love of God, could you please keep that kiss on the down-low," he whispered and leaned in. "I don't want anyone getting ideas about why she was hired."

"It's nobody's business, but why did you hire her?"

Jamie was silent for a moment. Why had he hired her? He wanted to say that it was strictly professional. That he knew she would be a competent assistant and nothing more. But he couldn't bring himself to tell his friend that. So he went with the partial truth. "She came highly recommended by Dr. Carmichael, and I trust his opinion," he said with a wave. "What happened here that night is just a wacky coincidence. She told me that it was a dare. Her friend Abby was trying to get her to be a little wilder, so she dared Maya to kiss me. That's all. That's the story."

"Uh-huh." Trevor stood straight, clearly unconvinced, and gestured to the empty glass Jamie had slammed down on the bar. "So, why the drink?"

"Why can't I have a drink in my own club?" he angrily defended himself. "I have to head back upstairs for a conference call soon, and I just wanted a quick break to relax a little. Is that okay with you?"

Trevor smiled at his friend's outburst. "It's fine, dude. If anyone needs to relax a little, it's clearly you."

4

MAYA ENTERED HER apartment at seven o'clock. She knew that Jamie was staying late for a conference call to settle some things with a presentation he would be giving at an upcoming conference in Las Vegas. She had offered to stay, but he dismissed her, saying it wasn't necessary. It still felt like a brush-off, all the same. She couldn't shake the feeling that he was uncomfortable being in the same room with her, and she wondered why he hired her if her presence made him so bristly? She made her way to the kitchen and poured herself a glass of Merlot, and when Abby ran into the kitchen to greet her she poured one for her friend, as well.

"So, how was your day?" Abby asked her, eager anticipation spread across her face.

Unsurprisingly, Abby had been supportive of Maya accepting the position. She was a great friend and she was so excited for Maya. She had even helped her decide on an outfit for her first day, in addition to helping her research Jamie and J. Sellers Holdings.

Maya's smile was tired. "It was long. There's a lot of work to get done. He's got so much going on. But—big news—he did tell me that the two of us would be going to Las Vegas in a few of weeks for a convention. So that's pretty exciting."

"Vegas? With Mr. Gorgeous? That's amazing. I'm so jealous! I love Vegas."

"Yeah, it should be great. I've never been there, but I doubt I'll get much time to sightsee, or shop, or anything else. He's pretty serious about business being strictly that." She took a sip of her wine.

"And a weird thing. The day was going fine at first, but then it's like his personality changed," she told Abby, frowning. "He spent most of the day ignoring me, and we both worked quietly at our desks. It was kind of awkward."

"You said he was busy. That's probably just him in work mode," Abby offered.

Maya rolled her eyes, embarrassed that she had been so sensitive. "Of course, that's it. He is busy. He's still at the office on a conference call, as we speak."

"Or, maybe he was just on edge because he was concerned you would jump him at his desk?" Abby mused, an evil glint in her eye. "Did you think about that?"

Maya sighed and brushed past her. "I don't know why I even talk to you."

"Because I'm your best friend and you value my opinion."

"Oh, right, I forgot," she laughed.

Abby followed her down the narrow hallway which led to the bedrooms and the bathroom. "He is insanely good-looking. Do you want to jump him at his desk?"

"No, I'm his assistant. This is a *strictly professional* working relationship."

"Maya, I know everything about you, so don't think

I don't know when you're all hot and bothered over a guy," she reminded her. "Even if it's been more than a millennium since that has happened."

Maya dropped her laptop bag and her purse in her bedroom and moved past Abby once again. "I'm not all *hot and bothered* over Jamie. But I am getting in the bath. I'll see you in a bit."

MAYA WALKED INTO the bathroom and shut the door, leaving Abby alone in the hallway. She turned on the hot water, letting it fall over her fingertips. Sitting on the edge of the tub, she poured in some bath salts and her favorite lavender bubble bath. She grabbed her phone and found a soft jazz radio station to stream online. Closing her eyes, Maya sipped her wine, finally able to decompress after her long day. When the tub filled, she lit some candles, and she quickly undressed and slipped into the too-hot water. The sensation made her hiss at first, drawing in air between her teeth. But she quickly acclimated and slid into the water until it covered the tops of her breasts.

She moaned. There was truly nothing better to her than a piping-hot bath. The bathtub was her sanctuary. It always had been. Even when she was younger, she looked forward to her private bath time. In the tub, she didn't have to think about her parents or the pressure they had put on her, her schoolwork, piano or her skating lessons. It was her time.

Closing her eyes, and without any other distractions, she let herself once again think of Jamie Sellers. As impossible as it was, she could still smell his cologne, feel him nearby, hear the deep timbre of his voice as it echoed in her brain.

All day, she had wanted to just reach out and touch him and run her fingertips over the coarse hair on his strong jaw. She remembered with a shiver the point in the afternoon when he had loosened his tie and unfastened the top button of his shirt. She wanted nothing more than to reach out and play with the small tuft of dark hair that was revealed. She tried not to stare as he rolled up his sleeves, exposing his strong, tan forearms and more hair that looked so exquisitely soft.

With a small sigh, Maya laid her head back against her bath pillow. There was no denying it. Abby was right, though she would never admit it. She did want Jamie. Badly. She was indeed all *hot and bothered.* It had been so long since she had thought that way about a man. She assumed now that she was basically finished with school she would have time for lust and desire and to give in to her romantic inclinations. She dismissed the thought as quickly as it formed. She would have wanted Jamie even if she was still in the freshman year of her MBA.

But after today, he had more than made it clear that he wanted nothing to do with her, outside of a professional, working relationship. The lack of interest he'd shown her was formidable, but that didn't mean she couldn't still be attracted to him. She would pine for him in secret if she needed to. Maya needed the job, and she wouldn't do anything to screw it up. But, God, he invaded her thoughts like no other.

Maya touched her own lips and remembered what it felt like to kiss him. She brought those fingertips to her jawline and down the sensitive skin of her neck. How would his lips feel tracing a similar route? She brushed her hand over her chest and down her full breasts. She smoothed her fingers over a stiff nipple and her fingers continued their voyage south over her belly.

When Maya reached the small triangle of curls at the apex of her thighs, she hesitated briefly before slipping a finger inside her warm folds. She bit back a moan when her digit skirted over the sensitive nub. She pictured Jamie's mouth and fingers on her, giving her the pleasure she sought with her own hand. She slipped one finger and then another inside, while her other hand strummed rhythmically around her clit. When she closed her eyes, she pictured Jamie's warmth was all around her, and he plunged into her. Waves, both physical and metaphorical, cascaded over her. Her legs shook, and she hooked one over the edge of the bathtub. Somewhere in her brain, she knew she was splashing water on the floor, but she didn't care. The pleasure that Jamie-in-her-head was giving her was too great to stop because of a little water on the floor. She felt herself rise and crest, and Maya pulled her bottom lip between her teeth in order to stop herself from screaming as she came with a force she'd never experienced in her life. She extracted her hand, and she leaned back in the tub until most of her face was under water.

I can do this, she told herself, with a sigh. *I can do this*.

5

JAMIE PUT THE finishing touches on his PowerPoint presentation, and he sat back in his chair, satisfied that it was finally ready. The upcoming trip to Las Vegas was a critical turning point for him, personally and professionally, and he couldn't leave anything to chance. He hadn't told anyone of his plans to expand his hotel and nightclub empire into the United States, and he knew that the Las Vegas Strip would be the place to start if he wanted to make an entrance people would notice. He drummed his fingers. He had lined up meetings with some very influential business contacts; people he would consider allies and competitors as soon as he brought his company to the Strip. He still needed to add one name to his list of appointments: Garrett Collins. So far, Collins hadn't taken any of Jamie's calls, and that frustrated him to no end.

He thought about the presentations and workshops that he and Maya would be attending during the conference. This trip would also be an extremely good opportunity for her as well, and he developed their schedule so they could attend the events most beneficial to her in her career path. He knew that being in a city like Vegas would prove to be a constant temptation to him, and he was certain that he wouldn't have taken the risk of inviting her if he absolutely didn't need her there with him.

Maya, he sighed. It had been several weeks since he had hired her. And he had done his best to keep her at arm's length. He had succeeded for the most part. But every minute he spent with her took every fragment of restraint that he could conjure up to not reach out and pull her to him. But he refrained. He didn't want to do anything to make her quit, and touching her, or kissing her, or lifting her onto his desk to make love to her would definitely do that. She was an excellent assistant, and he didn't want to screw this up.

His thoughts were interrupted when Mary walked into the office. "Jamie, I've got the travel arrangements made for you both for the Vegas trip."

Jamie looked up from his desk, as he pictured Maya lying naked on it. He exhaled, not daring to stand to meet his receptionist. "Thanks, Mary. Details?"

"You and Maya fly out next Monday morning. And you're both staying at the Bellagio. Jamie, you've got a suite, in case you plan on hosting any meetings or entertaining," she added with a wink. Jamie laughed. Mary had been with him for so long, and even though she was older, they still shared a close friendship. She knew that there was no truth to any of the tabloid gossip that was spread about Jamie, but it certainly didn't stop her from poking fun at him from time to time.

"Sounds good. What about Maya?" he asked innocently, knowing that if her bedroom was nearby, she would prove to be a distraction to him.

Mary smiled indulgently, sharp eyes glinting. "Not

to worry, Jamie. She's booked in a regular room. But it's still quite nice. Several floors below yours, even. So don't worry, your virtue is safe."

Jamie's mouth fell open. How did she know what he was just thinking? "What do you mean?"

Mary clicked her tongue. "Jamie, I've known you and worked closely with you for around a decade." She laughed at his gaping mouth and sat in a chair opposite his desk. "I'm afraid I know you better than you know yourself. I see how you both look at each other. And don't think Trevor didn't tell me about that kiss," she finished, with an eyebrow raised pointedly.

"Of course he did." Jamie sighed, fingers in his hair. "Remind me to thank him for that later. There's nothing between Maya and me," he stated, lying to her and himself.

Mary looked at him, unflinchingly. "And, Jamie, I can tell you're freezing her out. You don't treat her like you do other people here. She's a nice girl, so be good to her. You could do a lot worse for yourself."

He would have given her his classic it's-a-professional-relationship-and-that's-all rebuttal had Maya not breezed into the office at that moment. He remained seated. He knew it wasn't polite to sit when a woman entered the room, but behind his desk, he was still rock hard from his earlier fantasies of Maya. Thank God Mary had booked them on separate floors. Hopefully that would be enough. He would hate to have to ask Mary to rebook her at a different hotel…maybe off the strip…or out of the state. Basically as far away from his hotel as possible.

"Hello, Maya," Mary said brightly, standing from her chair.

"Hi, Mary. How are you?"

"I'm just grand, dear," she replied. "I was just telling Jamie that I've got your Vegas itinerary all ready. Jamie, I'll email them to you both."

"Thanks, Mary," he replied as she left and closed the door behind her.

MAYA SAT QUICKLY at her desk, blanching slightly. While she was excited about going to the convention in Las Vegas, she was not looking forward to spending five entire days alone with Jamie. Every day, she resolved to keep a hands-off attitude in her relationship with him. He was still cold to her, but she tried not to let it bother her. It seemed to be the way he did business, although, she had seen him interacting with other employees, and he was always kind and compassionate. It was curious, but she had already spent so much of her day thinking about and lusting over Jamie, she tried not to spend any more time worrying about it, lest she not get anything done at all.

"So, Vegas. Can't wait." She plastered a phony smile on her face and faced him from across the office.

"Yeah," he replied coolly. "Ever been before?"

"No, never. I actually haven't traveled much. I've been so busy with school and everything. Plus I don't really like flying."

A curt nod was his only response before he looked back down at his desk and resumed his work. He was silent until he sighed heavily.

"Everything okay?"

He looked up, almost surprised that she was even still in the room. It appeared as if she had caught him in a moment of weakness and he looked embarrassed. "Yeah. Well, no. I'm trying to arrange a meeting with Garrett

Collins." When she furrowed her brow, he elaborated. "He owns about 40 percent of the resort properties in Las Vegas. I want a sit down with him while we're there. But he won't even take my calls."

Maya's eyes widened in surprise. North of the border, when Jamie Sellers spoke, people listened. Canada's top businessmen and pillars of his industry were always eager to sit down with him, and the fact that Garrett Collins was not, surprised them both.

Pushing out of her chair, Maya walked to Jamie's desk. "What did you want to see him about?"

He paused. "Well, it can't hurt to have an ally in Las Vegas, especially one as formidable as Garrett Collins. I thought we could just have a conversation. About the city and the business."

Maya raised an eyebrow. She could tell that Jamie was being intentionally vague. But she wouldn't push it. If Jamie needed to meet with Garrett Collins, he had his reasons. She leaned over his chair, hovering over his shoulder. The smell of his cologne stirred her senses and she faltered slightly, unintentionally allowing her suddenly heavy breasts to skim the top of his shoulder. She thought it to be a curious reaction when she felt him stiffen slightly below her, and she saw him close his eyes for just a second.

Jamie cleared his throat and turned slightly to face her. "What are you doing?"

She picked over a few things on his desk, suddenly feeling bold. She wanted to help him. To prove to him that he hadn't made a mistake in hiring her. "I'm looking for this guy's number," she told him.

"Maya, no. You can't just call him and request a meeting."

She picked up a piece of paper and studied the numbers scrawled over it. "Is this it?"

Jamie looked at the paper, as she still hovered over his shoulder. "Yeah. It's his office number. His assistant Andre keeps stonewalling me. He says there's absolutely no time for him to see me."

Maya scoffed and picked up Jamie's phone. She perched on the corner of his desk and crossed her legs, dialing the number. "Let's just see about that," she said and winked at him.

"What are you going to do?" he asked her warily. He was nervous about whatever she had planned. He saw the mischief and the wicked smile etched on her face.

"I'm just going to call him. Maybe I'll have a little more luck, assistant to assistant.

"Garrett Collins's office, this is Andre."

JAMIE SAT BACK in his chair, fingers locked behind his head. He smiled at Maya as she started talking to the person on the other end, presumably Collins's assistant.

"Hi, Andre," she said, her voice smooth. "My name is Maya Connor and I'm calling from Jamie Sellers's office in Montreal. How are you?" She paused. "That's great to hear. I'm doing well also…Well, I'd be better if you could possibly find time for our bosses to meet while we're in Vegas next week…Andre," she laughed. "We're all busy, I'm sure Mr. Collins is preparing for his annual shareholders meeting, and judging from the rumors of an audit committee investigation I've been reading about he'll want to have some good news to bring with him to placate the shareholders. And I believe a meeting with Mr. Sellers might provide just the remedy for skittish investors. It'll be a show that he is looking to meet with a young, impressive businessman. But all Mr. Sellers is looking for is a brief sit-down. Twenty minutes. A drink in his suite, perhaps, that's all."

Jamie watched Maya as she broke into a huge smile. "Andre, you are a prince. Thank you so much!"

Jamie sat up straight in his chair. *What did she just do?*

Maya reached across Jamie's desk and grabbed his pen and she scribbled a time and date on the notepad near her hip. "Great. I guess we'll be seeing you and Mr. Collins in Vegas next week," she signed off before hanging up the phone.

Jamie stared at her, unable to believe that she had come through for him and had managed to do something that he'd been unable to. She had arranged a meeting for him with Garrett Collins. He shook his head at her in amazement. "So?"

Maya laughed lightly. "Well, I just got you forty-five minutes with Garrett Collins on Wednesday night. In your suite."

"Are you kidding me?" he exclaimed, grabbing her shoulders and pulling her into a hug. "That's incredible! Thank you so much, Maya!"

She laughed again. "I'm glad I could help."

They stood in his office, caught in an embrace, his arms tight around her waist and her hands warm on his shoulders. His resolution to not touch her had snapped and he couldn't help himself. Jamie buried his face in the crease of her neck and shoulder. He inhaled, smelling her shampoo. The hug went on a beat too long. And Jamie felt Maya pull away slowly. He watched her face. The emotion in her eyes ranging from surprise, awareness, to desire, and he was sure that the same feelings were mirrored in his own.

This was the first time since the night in the club that he had even let himself get physically near Maya. He'd always kept her at arm's length because he knew that this would happen. He would touch her and not be able to stop. He was unable to pull away, his hands moved to the small of her back, and he pulled her closer to him, pressing the hard length of his erection against her belly.

She moaned softly in encouragement. "Jamie," she whispered.

With a groan, he leaned in. His lips were just a breath away from hers when the phone on her desk rang. They broke apart and both looked at the offending phone.

Maya looked at Jamie. She was flushed and her pupils were dilated, just a thin sliver of color showed around the black. "I'd better get that."

"Yeah." Jamie exhaled, releasing her, so she could run back to her desk.

That was close. Jamie knew that if he had let himself kiss her, he wouldn't have been able to stop it. The kiss wouldn't have ended until they were both naked and heaving atop his desk. He would have taken her, without any thought to the repercussions. He ran a hand through his hair and grabbed his jacket from the back of his chair. And with a quick wave to Maya as she spoke on the phone, he left the office, and he didn't return until the next morning.

6

"AND THIS IS going to be the spa," Jamie told Maya as he opened the door to a large, dusty room and ushered her inside. He was taking her on a tour of the foreclosed hotel property he had bought in downtown Montreal, the one that he was in the process of rebuilding and renovating to turn it into the first Swerve Hotel.

"It used to be a ballroom," he explained, taking a look around the expansive room. "It's the only space big enough to install all of the features we want in the spa, and we're going to renovate some old guest rooms to make smaller event and conference spaces."

He watched her eyes survey the room, no doubt envisioning all that he did when he looked around the old hotel. "Jamie," she whispered. "This is going to be incredible."

He smiled. He wasn't sure why, but her belief in him made him feel relief.

Since the day she had arranged his meeting with Garrett Collins, he and Maya had enjoyed an easier camaraderie, which was nice, because the amount of time they had been spending together in the office had increased drastically since her first week. They often worked fourteen-hour days, side by side. He decided that he had to learn to be in the same room with her without being cold and distant or, on the flip side, throwing her on his desk and completely ravishing her. Sure, he still wanted her, but he had developed coping mechanisms to deal with her proximity, most notably his new daily three-cold-showers routine, but so far it was working.

He escorted her out of the future spa and down the long hallway to the lobby door.

"When do you think we can get underway on the construction?"

We. Jamie's stomach fluttered at the thought of undertaking this project with Maya at his side. He cleared his throat roughly, while bringing a hand to his hair. "I'm hoping we can have all of the permits sorted out in a couple of weeks. There's a lot of work to do, but I'm planning to open by October, to make an impact during the fall and winter tourist seasons."

She whistled. "That's very ambitious. But if anyone's capable of it, it's you."

"It's us," he corrected, then cleared his throat. "I mean, the team. As a whole we aren't afraid of some hard work." He dragged his fingers through his hair.

Maya looked at him out of the corner of her eye, an amused smile playing on her lips. "You do that a lot, you know?"

Jamie looked down at her. "I do what a lot?" They were at his car and he stopped at the passenger-side door and opened it for her.

"You run your fingers through your hair. A lot. Is it a nervous tic?"

Hmm. Jamie had never realized that he had any such habit. "I do?"

"Yeah, I've noticed it. It's cute, in fact," she said, lowering to sit in the sunken seat of the sports car.

He closed the door after her, and when he saw a man walking toward his car in the empty parking lot, he frowned.

John Power, the gossip hound disguised as a reporter who seemed to follow Jamie's every move. "Jamie," he said with a smile. But he was anything but friendly. "I thought that was your car."

Jamie sighed. "What can I do for you, Power?"

He shrugged. "Just wondering what you're doing in the neighborhood. I heard that you bought this hotel. Just wondering if you wanted to give me an exclusive? Tell me what you're planning for the space."

"Why would I tell you any of that, exactly?"

"Or, you can tell me the name of the gorgeous woman sitting in your car."

Jamie lost it. He pushed the man against the car and bent him back over the roof. He noticed Maya get out of the car.

"Jamie, what's going on?"

"Get back in the car, Maya," he commanded her.

"Should I call the police?"

"No," he told her, releasing John. "He was just leaving." Jamie pushed him away from the driver's-side door, out of his way. He pulled it open and got inside.

Before Jamie could close the door, he heard John laugh. "I'll see you around, Jamie." He bent and looked into the car, waving at Maya through the open door. "Smile, Maya." He held up his camera and snapped a picture of her.

"Fucking sleaze," Jamie muttered, opening his door, fire in his eyes. Now the man had involved Maya, and that was unacceptable. Jamie would show him. Before he could fully get out of the car, Power had run out of the parking lot. "Coward," he muttered, as he stood beside his car.

"Jamie, ignore him," Maya called from the passenger's seat. "It's not worth it."

He got back into his car and slammed the door shut with a force that shook the car. "I'm sorry about that, Maya. He shouldn't have taken your picture," he told her and quickly put his car in gear. He sped out of the parking lot and into the road.

"Who was that guy?" Maya asked. She could see how the tension racked Jamie's body, as he had a white-knuckle grip on the wheel. She had never seen Jamie lose his cool like that. He was normally so calm and in control of his emotions. This Jamie, this fuming, heavy-breathing beast sitting next to her was not the Jamie Sellers she knew. She was also feeling unsettled that that strange man had taken her picture.

Jamie didn't answer her right away.

"Jamie?"

He took a deep breath. "That was John Power," he said. "Resident scumbag reporter. He's always on my ass, hounding me."

"Why?"

He was silent.

"You can tell me, Jamie. Why is he after you?"

"Well, it all started when I opened my first club. I told you I was a troublemaker. It didn't go away overnight just because I reached some level of success. I worked hard, but I partied hard, as well. I was always being photographed stumbling drunk coming out of my own club or caught in inappropriate situations with women. I had too much, too soon, and I was a real mess," he sighed.

"So, anyway, one night I was sitting in the VIP booth at Swerve. I was sitting with some lingerie models— how's that for a cliché?—and we were drinking, some drugs were passed around and pretty soon I'm making out with one of the women, her top is undone and my hand is up her skirt."

Maya had heard that story before. She had seen the pictures on the internet. Still, as she heard him retell the story to her, the remorse and regret etched over his face, she felt for him. She put a comforting hand on his forearm. He turned his eyes from the road to look at her with surprise. "Then what happened? How does John Power fit into that?"

"He was there. We don't normally allow press into the club. But he was new, unknown, and he snapped the now-famous pics of me and the model. From what I gathered, he then sold them for a pretty substantial amount of money. Since that night, he's basically been my shadow. He takes pictures of me and he pairs them with a salacious story, and bam, more money for him. I guess he considers me to be his cash cow. But the hell of it is, I don't even get to have any of the fun he accuses me of, now do I?" He laughed without humor.

"I'm sorry that happened to you, Jamie. That guy is a snake. He might not go away any time soon. But I think the more important part of the story is that you cleaned up your act. You're a complete success, and nothing is going to change that, certainly not some gross *news* stories. We can ignore him. There's bigger fish to fry."

He smiled at her, his dazzling white teeth making her flutter a little. "Thanks, Maya, I really appreciate it."

"And besides," she continued, "we all do stupid things when we're drinking. In fact, once, my friend Abby got me drunk and dared me to kiss some random guy in a bar." She laughed, and Jamie laughed with her. She sat back in her seat. She was glad that her business relationship was becoming more relaxed. Her thoughts turned to the old hotel that she had just toured. She couldn't wait until they started work on it, and she couldn't wait to be part of the finished product.

7

MAYA PUSHED THE heavy door open using her hip as she held two large coffee cups in her hands—a latte for herself and a red-eye for Jamie. She often worried about his caffeine intake as he would surely have at least three more before he went home for the evening.

He looked up at her with a broad smile. *Smiling at me? Or the coffee?* "Maya, you are a goddess. Thank you so much."

"It was nothing," she told him. "I know that if I came in holding only the one that you would just spend your day pouting."

He stood and met her in the middle of the office. "I don't pout," he argued.

"No," she laughed, passing him his coffee. "You scowl."

He took his cup with a laugh of his own. She felt her stomach flutter whenever he flashed those pearly whites at her. Those smiles had become more common in the past few weeks. They had apparently reached some sort of unspoken truce. He was no longer as cold and distant as he had been when she'd been hired.

They were finally able to joke and laugh together and have actual conversations that had nothing to do with work. They were getting to know each other as people and she and Jamie had become friends. Friends with moderate—*okay, extreme*—amounts of sexual tension.

She watched intently as he brought the cup to his lips. They may have become friendly, but as she remembered the night she kissed him, she found herself jealous of the plastic coffee lid. She quickly turned away, lest he catch the flush that stained her cheeks. When she sat at her desk, Jamie approached her instead of returning to his own desk.

"Do you have plans on Saturday?" he asked her.

Plans? she thought. "No, I don't think I do."

He sat on the corner of her desk and sipped from his cup. "I'm having a barbecue, well, a pool party I guess, at my place on Saturday afternoon. It's something I do every year, to mark the beginning of summer. But it's just a few friends. It's going to be pretty laid-back. You should come."

A pool party at Jamie's? Hanging out with Jamie outside of work, seeing him having fun…in swim trunks? It was an opportunity that Maya couldn't possibly pass up… Except she had to. She smacked her forehead. "Oh, shoot! I can't!"

Jamie frowned. "Really?"

"Yeah, I promised Abby that we would hang out. She's been kind of depressed lately. She's having trouble with the old job hunt."

"Bring her along," Jamie proposed. "She's welcome."

"I can't impose—"

"It's no imposition at all. It's a party. The more, the merrier."

Maya picked up her cell phone. "Great! I'll text her now. Thanks!"

Two DAYS LATER, Maya and Abby pulled up to Jamie's condo building. She'd known it would be swanky and high-end, but she'd had no idea how luxurious it was. Prestige Towers rose more than twenty stories into the sky. A valet in a blue jacket approached Abby's old car and opened the doors for them, and then got behind the wheel and drove it toward an underground parking lot.

"I hope he was actually a valet," Abby quipped, watching her car drive out of sight. "And that he didn't steal my car to strip it and sell the parts..."

Maya laughed. "If thieves were looking to steal a car from this building, I don't think your fifteen-year-old Corolla would be the big score."

"Hey, Carol's been good to us!" Abby protested, in defense of the car they had named Carol the Corolla.

"You're right, I apologize." Maya smiled at the doorman, and they entered the lobby.

"Wow," Maya muttered as they took in the large expanse of marble that constituted the floor, the walls, probably the ceiling and most definitely the large desk that was placed square in the middle. The art pieces on the wall all seemed to be original works of art that she recognized. "He lives here?"

"He's a gazillionaire, of course he does," was Abby's quick response.

"I knew that he's rich, but I didn't realize he had this kind of money." Maya looked around in disbelief at the sheer opulence of the place.

Abby looked over at her and turned to face her. "Maya. Chill. Close your mouth, play it cool, or they'll know we don't belong here and they'll kick us out." She laughed.

"Okay, I'm playing it cool," Maya responded. They walked casually to the desk and the unhappy-looking man sitting behind it. "We're here to see Jamie Sellers," she told him.

"Is he expecting you?" he said with boredom, glancing at a list of names on the computer in front of him.

"Yes, he is. We're Maya Connor and Abby Shaw."

He sighed and checked the list again. He tapped the touch screen next to their names and they changed color from black to green. "All right, ladies." He pushed himself up from his stool. It was apparent that he would rather be doing anything at all than escorting women to a rich, handsome man's life-of-luxury pool party. "Follow me, please." He led them to a smaller elevator located in an alcove off the main lobby. "This elevator will take you directly to Mr. Sellers's penthouse suite." They got inside and he inserted a key and pushed a series of buttons and the doors closed in front of them.

The elevator ride was surprisingly a quick one. Apparently, people who live in the penthouses don't have time to take elevators that travel at a regular speed. And when the doors opened up into his foyer, she was shocked to see the huge, loft-style apartment before her. It was tastefully decorated, and very much a man's space. Lots of dark leather and wood, clean and spacious. But the huge windows, which provided an incredible view of the city, made the place feel light. Maya inhaled deeply. It smelled like Jamie… She looked around, wondering how many times he had entertained women in his condo.

Probably tons. A guy like Jamie. This place must be a regular panty-dropper for most women.

"Get a load of this place." Abby's voice broke into her thoughts. "I didn't think people actually lived like this. It's pretty crazy, hey?"

"It really is," Maya agreed.

"Hey!" Jamie called out to them. "You made it."

He walked into his kitchen through the sliding door that led outside, most likely to the pool area. He was wearing a loose-fitting white tank top over a pair of red board shorts, and completing the ensemble were the most worn pair of boat shoes she had ever seen. This was the most casual she had ever seen Jamie. He looked relaxed, for once, and he wore a huge smile on his face.

"I'm glad you came."

Maya could barely speak. She was so taken aback by Jamie's casual appearance that she stuttered slightly. "Uh, th-thanks. Thanks for the invitation." Then she said nothing and just stared at him for a few seconds, until she felt Abby's sharp elbow jab her ribs. She had completely forgotten that her friend was standing next to her, waiting for an introduction.

"Oh! Jamie, this is my friend Abby. Abby, Jamie."

Jamie extended his hand to Abby. "Nice to meet you, Abby. Do I know you from somewhere?" He thought about it for a second. "Oh, of course, Dr. C.'s class. When I gave that talk. You were sitting next to Maya, right?"

"That's right." Abby smiled. "It was a great lecture."

Jamie winced. "Ooh, I don't like that word. Makes me sound all old and stodgy." He laughed, and in a move completely uncharacteristic of Jamie Sellers, he turned and put an arm around the shoulders of both Maya and Abby. "Well, ladies, shall we hit the party?"

"Sounds good to me," Abby answered.

Maya closed her eyes and relished in the feeling of Jamie's arm around her. "Me, too," she said as he led them outside.

8

JAMIE TOOK A beer from the fridge he'd had installed as part of a poolside bar and popped it open. He loved the outdoor oasis that he'd created on the terrace of his condo. He had meticulously planned the space for the pool, the hot tub, the bar, lounge area, even down to the plants and flowers adorning it, the foliage that afforded him and his guests all the privacy that they needed. Sure, it was June and it might have been a little chilly for an outdoor party, but with the warmth of the pool and carefully placed exterior heaters, nobody complained. He loved his outdoor area, but because of all the time he spent working, he rarely got to enjoy it, or any of the other luxuries he could now afford because of his hard work and success. *A sad irony.*

He watched his guests mill about the poolside. They were all smiling, having fun. He really missed just spending time with his friends and the people he loved. He had no real family, but the dozen or so people who congregated around the pool, he considered them to be his true family.

His eyes were drawn to Maya as she pulled herself out

of the water. She was wearing an orange bikini. When he invited her to a pool party, he knew that she would most definitely be wearing a bathing suit. But he couldn't have imagined how she would look in that two-piece. From behind his dark aviators, he watched her pick up a towel and use it to dry herself off, as she made her way to the loungers that she and Abby had occupied. He could see the rivulets of water as they rolled down her olive skin—down her breasts, over her smooth, flat tummy, trailing the longest legs he'd ever seen on a woman. She leaned over and said something to Abby, and they both laughed.

Abby. The woman who had dared her to kiss him in the club. *I should really buy that woman a present.* He'd almost mentioned the night he'd watched them at Swerve when they'd been formally introduced earlier, and he'd had to bite his tongue. But he knew that it probably would have embarrassed Maya if he'd mentioned it. However, without Abby's intervention that night in the club, Maya wouldn't have stumbled into his life, and only after a month, he now couldn't imagine his life without her in it.

"Hey, man, what's occupying all of your attention?" Trevor came up behind Jamie and slapped him on the back. He figured out where Jamie's gaze was fixed. On Maya. He smiled. "Ahh," he said, understanding.

"What?"

"You're checking out Maya."

Busted. Jamie shook his head in denial. "Nope."

"Her cute, little, blonde friend, then."

"Absolutely not."

Trevor grinned. "Can I assume you're going to ask both of them to stay after the party and help you *clean up*?"

"Oh, come on, Trevor," Jamie reprimanded him.

Trevor put both hands up in protest. "Hey, it's something that you would have done 10 years ago, I'm just saying."

It was true. Partier Jamie wouldn't have passed up the opportunity to try to get both of them into bed, separately or together, it wouldn't have mattered to him. But now, he had little time or energy for the extracurricular activities he'd once so wholeheartedly enjoyed. But as he watched Maya lie down on the lounger enjoying the heat of the sun, he felt his interest rising. Her long, lean body was stretched out in repose, glistening with the sunscreen she had applied. His mouth watered at just the sight of her.

He wanted her. No doubt about that. But there was no way in hell that he could have her. She was his assistant. It would be terribly unprofessional, against his company rules. And if it didn't work out, he would lose one of the best assistants he'd ever had. He dragged his fingers through his hair in frustration. He turned to Trevor who was also watching Maya and Abby as they lay by the pool, sunning their bodies.

"Think she'll give me her number?" Trevor asked him.

Jamie scowled and turned to his friend. "Maya?"

"No. Do you think I'm crazy? I mean Abby. She's cute, right?"

Jamie looked, but he could barely see Abby. His attention was riveted on Maya. "Yeah, I guess."

MAYA SPREAD OUT on the lounger she had selected. She closed her eyes and let the sun warm her body. Behind her sunglasses, she cast a covert glance toward Jamie. He was standing by the bar, talking with Trevor. They were looking at her and Abby. They tried to hide their stares behind sunglasses, but she could tell. *Men are so obvious*. She smiled and turned her head toward Abby.

"I think you have an admirer," she told her.

Abby took a sip of her frozen concoction that Trevor had whipped up for her. "Mmm, that's good. What are you talking about?"

"Trevor, he's looking right at you."

"Really?" Abby full-on turned her head toward them and waved, wiggling her fingers at the men. Trevor raised a hand in return with a smile. "He is quite cute. But Jamie is the one who can't keep his eyes off you."

She took another quick look at Jamie. He had taken off his tank top and he stood there, his low-slung board shorts hanging just below his lean hips. She wondered when he had the time to work out, with the crazy hours he worked, but he clearly found the time. His broad shoulders led to a firm chest, and the fine hair that covered him spread over well-formed pecs down to defined abdominal muscles. He was a feast for the eyes, but somehow her attention was fastened to the pronounced diagonal lines of his pelvic bone, which disappeared under the red shorts.

Maya turned back to Abby and she shook her head. "No. He's made it abundantly clear that he isn't interested in me like that. Plus, he's my boss. It just can't happen."

"You're both adults. I don't see why you both can't mix a little business and pleasure. It'll certainly make all of those long nights you've been working with him more interesting."

"Never going to happen, Abby," she muttered. No matter how much she wanted it to.

THE SUN STARTED its descent in the sky and began to cast shadows over Jamie's patio. People said their goodbyes and filtered out. Maya, Abby and Trevor remained. But when they started gathering their things, Jamie walked up to them. He was unfortunately once again shirted.

"Maya," he called, looking reluctant. "Do you mind sticking around for a bit? I hate to do this but I got an email about Vegas and there's something we need to hammer out with my presentation." It seemed that casual Jamie couldn't stick around for long. Jamie Sellers, mogul/boss, had made a reappearance.

She pulled her sundress over her head, and she nodded. "Yeah, sure. Do we have to head to the office?"

"No. We should be able to handle it from my home office."

Maya turned to Abby. "Do you mind if I stay for a little while?"

"Not at all. I'm actually going to get a cab home and come back for my car tomorrow. I think I've had a few too many of Trevor's margaritas."

Maya nodded at her friend's wobbly state. "That's good. Okay, I'll see you at home."

Trevor came up behind the group, and Maya noticed when he put a hand on the small of Abby's back. "I'll walk you down."

Abby smiled at him. "Thanks."

Jamie and Maya watched Trevor and Abby walk out. When they said goodbye, Jamie extended an arm, ushering Maya down a hallway. "Shall we get to work?"

9

THEY HAD WORKED for hours when Jamie finally looked up
from his laptop. "Maya, I think we're done." He rubbed
the back of his neck. He was suddenly exhausted. His
fatigue was probably a combination of the sun he'd got
earlier, the few beers he'd had and the fact that he had
spent several hours staring at his computer screen.

There had been a problem with one of the sections of
his presentation. Some numbers in his projections didn't
add up. It was something that had to be fixed right away,
before his presentation in Vegas. He couldn't afford to
look like a fool, and he was glad that his team had caught
it in time. *And thank God for Maya.* She had agreed to
stay and work with him. She didn't have to stay, but she
didn't hesitate in saying yes.

"Your neck okay?" He looked up and found Maya
looking at him. She was still wearing her bathing suit
under her sundress, and the smell of her coconut sunscreen hit his nose. He could see red on her cheeks and
nose; he assumed that she must have gotten a little too
much sun that afternoon.

He smiled at her concern. "Yeah, I'm just a little stiff

from sitting here." He winced. "I might be tempted to get in the hot tub later."

"That sounds like heaven," she commented absently, thumb swiping across the screen of her phone.

He looked at her beautiful form sitting across his desk. A terrible idea occurred to him. "Why not join me?"

That got her attention. She looked up. "I'm sorry. What was that?"

This was his opportunity to take back what he'd said. To offer to call her a car and get her safely out of his condo before he made a mistake. But instead, he couldn't help but repeat the same awful, terrible, so-bad idea. "Join me. In the hot tub."

"Are you sure?" Maya sounded skeptical. Jamie regarded her closely. Was she just as worried as he was about the sexual tension that bubbled so closely to the surface of every interaction they shared?

"Yeah," he answered nonchalantly, mentally slapping himself. "Yeah, it's a big tub. I think we deserve to relax a little, don't you?"

She visibly exhaled. Jamie watched her breasts rise and fall with her breath. *This is a bad idea, Sellers. What is the matter with you?*

"Sure. It sounds great. Let's do it."

WHEN THEY WALKED back out to the terrace, the sun had fully set, and the automatic timer had turned on the exterior lights, so that the night was now cast in a yellow-orange glow. He had also forgotten to turn off the music. So now, instead of the pop and dance music that had been playing earlier, it had since slowed to R & B. *Nice romantic setting.* Jamie frowned. It was as if the Fates had conspired to usher him and the assistant he couldn't ever have into bed together.

This is such a bad idea. But it was too late to say anything. He couldn't invite her to relax with him and then turn around and kick her out. He took a deep breath. *Keep it in your pants, Sellers. That's all you need to do. You're a grown man. Act like it.*

The hot tub bubbled away furiously, steam rising into the chill of the night air. It looked as inviting as all hell. He watched as Maya pulled her dress over her head, and he shuddered inwardly as most of his blood rushed south. He turned away quickly, lest she see the effect she had on what was inside his shorts, and he busied himself at the bar.

"You want a drink or something?"

"Yeah, some water would be good," she told him, stepping into the hot water.

He opened the refrigerator to look for drinks, bottles of water, cans of soda—*anything!*—but he found nothing but a bottle of cold champagne. It seemed as if his guests had cleared out all of the nonalcoholic options.

"Are you kidding me?" he muttered at their only choice of beverage.

"Everything okay?" she asked, settling in the water and sitting back, closing her eyes.

"Yeah, but all I could find was this," he explained. Knowing that he was probably making yet another colossal mistake, he pulled out the bottle and held it aloft. "Champagne?"

He heard her sigh. *In resignation?* "Okay, I'll have a glass."

He scooped some ice into a bucket and put the bottle in it. Picking up two glasses he walked over to the hot tub and put everything on the edge. He got in and sat directly across from her. He shuddered with the feeling of the hot water scorching most of his skin. He moaned involuntarily. "I don't think I use this thing nearly enough." He poured a glass of champagne for each of them and passed hers over.

Their fingers touched and the contact sizzled throughout Jamie's body, shooting straight to his groin.

"Thanks." She accepted hers and sat straight against the edge of the tub, not looking at him.

He watched her. *That's a good way to play this*, Jamie considered. *I just won't look at her, speak to her or anything else. We can just sit here, enjoy the tub and ignore each other. I'll forget she's even here.*

"This really is great," she sighed.

There goes that plan. He kept his eyes closed. "Yeah, the hot tub was definitely a priority when I moved in here."

"Too bad you spend all of your time at the office," she commented.

"Yeah," he murmured. He was silent for a moment. "Listen, Maya, I really want to apologize for the way I treated you when I first hired you. I was rude and dismissive and I'm sorry."

Maya furrowed her brow. "Jamie, it's fine. I didn't mind, really. I just thought that you were too busy with work to deal with idle chitchat. Not that you needed to apologize. But apology accepted, anyway."

"Thank you." He smiled at her. "I'm just glad we can be friends, despite everything that's happened."

"Everything that's happened?" she questioned. "Do you mean the night I kissed you?"

His pulse sped up just at the memory of the kiss.

"Don't worry. That's so very much in the past," she said. "And, yeah, we are friends. Don't question it."

Jamie relaxed slightly. And he grinned at her. He was glad to have Maya in his corner. She was smart, charismatic, intuitive, beautiful, sexy… He shook his head and drank his champagne. He extended his glass to the center of the hot tub. "Maya, I would like to propose a toast to us, and to knocking 'em dead in Vegas."

She smiled and clinked her glass to his. "To knocking 'em dead."

MAYA HADN'T MEANT to drink so much champagne. Originally, she was just going to enjoy the hot water, have a glass of champagne, then get out, call a cab and get home. But when the cool bubbles of the champagne hit her tongue, she was suddenly parched. Her next sip was a gulp, as was the one after that and the one after that. Jamie was saying something to her, but she wasn't hearing any of the words. She was caught up watching the way his arms and shoulders flexed with every movement he made when he spoke, when he drank, when he locked his hands behind his head and leaned back in relaxation. *It should be illegal for a man to look this good.*

She loved to see him relaxed and smiling. She'd had fun at the party. She got to spend more time with him and Trevor and some more of their friends, and she'd taken some much-needed time to just relax and sit by the pool in the sunshine.

"Thanks for the invite today. Abby and I had so much fun. It was nice to relax."

"Well, it wouldn't have been the same without you. And Abby's pretty awesome. I see why you love her," he told her. "And Trevor seems to like her, as well."

She laughed lightly. "I noticed that. She's pretty easy to like."

"I'm happy that you guys had a good time."

"Jamie, can I ask you a question?"

"Of course."

"It might seem a little personal," she warned him.

"Well, why don't you ask it, and see if I answer it?"

She scooted a little closer to him, as if to demonstrate the personal nature of the question. "Why don't you get out of the office more? Have some fun?"

Jamie considered his answer. "Well, I told you about my reputation as Party Animal Jamie Sellers, but for the past ten years or so, I've been trying to keep it clean, keep my name out of the papers for bad behavior. I figured that the best way to stay out of trouble was to lock myself away in my office and bury myself in my work," he explained. "And being the hardest worker in the room just led to me needing to be the best. The more clubs I opened, the more I needed to open. The more successful I was, the more successful I needed to become." He shrugged his shoulders.

"But you're already so successful, and your charity work is so well-known, I think you can afford to take some days off, a little time away, maybe leave before five o'clock some days. You've earned it."

"Well, I think I just got into the habit of working so much. It's hard to break it."

Maya nodded. She understood the compulsion to be the best. It was something she had lived with all of her life. She imagined that she and Jamie were similar in many ways. Maybe that's why they got along so well.

When she didn't say anything for a while, he smiled. "But we're not really here to talk about work, are we?"

"I guess not," Maya laughed. She was sitting next to him, their shoulders touching as they sipped their champagne.

Jamie finished his glass, and instead of refilling it, he shrugged and brought the bottle to his mouth. He leaned his head back and took a swig. She watched the muscles in his throat work as he swallowed down the bubbly liquid. He passed her the bottle and she smiled.

"Thanks." She also took a mouthful. When she handed it back, he wasn't looking and his hand slipped, accidentally encircling her wrist. At the contact, her breath stopped. Her eyes caught his, and his grip on her tightened.

Jamie took the bottle from her hand and put it back on the edge of the hot tub, and with a slight tug, he brought her closer to him. She knew what he was doing but was powerless to change course, and then she sat directly on his lap. Under the water, he smoothed his palm over her two legs that were draped over one of his thighs. "Maya," he murmured, placing his other hand at the back of her neck. He pulled her to him, his lips crushing hers.

He kissed her hard and furious. And she wholly reciprocated. It was as if weeks of pent-up sexual frustration were let loose in one kiss. Her hands gripped his shoulders, as if she were holding on for dear life. And she was. The way Jamie kissed her might actually kill her.

He kept one hand on her ass while the other slid up her stomach and found her breast. With an impatient growl, he pushed her triangle top aside. He squeezed it gently and she gave a moan, which turned to a whimper when he pinched her nipple.

Jamie chuckled at her reaction and pulled away from her mouth, closing his lips on the rosy bud of her stiff nipple. He closed his lips around it and sucked lightly, lashing her with his tongue. She cried out at the sensation, and she brought her hand down to rest on his stiff length—*my God!* When his fingers found the strings of her bottoms, she finally came to her senses.

"Jamie, wait," she whispered, pulling away.

"What's wrong?"

"We can't do this," she told him, shimmying back to the other side of the tub. She hastily adjusted her bikini top. "I'm your assistant," she breathed. "You're my boss."

Jamie worked to catch his breath. "You're right. Shit, I'm sorry, Maya. I can't believe I did that."

"It's okay," she assured him. "We were both pretty much active participants there."

He spoke over her, looking into his open palms. "It must have been the champagne. We've had a lot to drink."

Maya nodded in agreement and quickly pushed herself out of the tub. In the cool night air, goose bumps rose on her skin. But she wasn't cold. Jamie's kiss and his touch had lit a fire in her very core. "I should go." She reached for a towel to dry herself off.

Jamie also got out. He didn't bother to hide the turgid erection he sported. It held her attention. It's not like its presence was any secret, she'd already felt it, wrapped her fingers around it.

"I'll call you a car."

She nodded and turned away. If she looked at him any longer, his strong, lean body, the impressive bulge in his trunks, she wouldn't be able to leave.

"That would be great. Thank you," she said quietly as he walked into his house.

10

"LADIES AND GENTLEMEN, welcome to Air Canada, flight 395, with nonstop service to Las Vegas, Nevada," the pilot's deep voice droned throughout the cabin. "We'll be pulling away from the gate shortly, and it looks like smooth flying all the way to Vegas. So settle in, get comfortable and please watch the following video about the safety features of this aircraft."

Jamie put his head back and closed his eyes. He was about to spend the next five hours sitting next to Maya. Since hiring her, he had attempted to keep his distance, for fear of reaching out and touching the hair that looked so luxuriously soft, or the smooth skin that beckoned to him. They hadn't discussed what had happened in his hot tub, both honoring their unspoken agreement to forget it happened, he supposed. But how could he forget her smooth skin, the noises she'd made when he turned her on. *Jesus, this is going to be a long trip.* He rubbed his eyes and sent a cautious glance at the beautiful woman next to him.

He was surprised to see the anxious, fearful expression that covered her face. "You okay, Maya?"

Keeping her head back in her seat, she turned slightly to look at him. "Yeah. It's kind of embarrassing really, but I'm kind of afraid of flying. I've been on enough planes, but I never like it."

Jamie smiled. "It's okay. But you know that flying is safer than driving, right?"

"That doesn't really help when there's engine trouble and you plummet to your death, instead of pulling over to the curb," she murmured as she closed her eyes.

He chuckled lightly. "Touché. Why don't you try to get some sleep?"

She shook her head quickly. "I can't sleep on a plane."

"We can get you some wine…?" he suggested, flagging down a flight attendant.

"Sure, but I can't drink alone. Will you have some, too?"

Would he have some wine? When he vividly remembered what happened the last time they'd had alcohol together. He would need a lot more than wine to get through this flight. He was close enough to smell her shampoo. The scent brought him back to that night, not to mention their near miss in his office. When he turned to her, he could see the flecks of gold in her otherwise dark eyes. He felt the heat of her arm next to his on the armrest. He wondered if the flight attendants had access to strong narcotics. That would be the only way he would get through this flight.

"Sure, I'll have a glass," he said and smiled at her. "I hope to get some sleep later on." He ordered them each a glass of wine. And when the flight attendant returned, they took their glasses and drank them in mouthfuls.

A COUPLE OF hours and some glasses of wine later, Maya felt herself jostle awake. She must have fallen asleep at some point during the flight, because her head was perched on Jamie's shoulder when she opened her eyes. How long had he let her sleep like that without waking her? She checked to make sure she hadn't drooled on him, but quickly forgot about that when she felt the plane shake violently.

She sat up straight and looked to Jamie, his face undeniably calm. "What's going on?" she asked him, grabbing and squeezing his armrest.

"Just a little turbulence," he assured her. "But it seems like you already slept through the worst of it." When the plane jolted again and she cried out softly, he placed a warm reassuring hand over hers. "It's okay, Maya. Just close your eyes."

His calm, sure voice and his hand over hers reassured her. She squeezed her eyes shut. "Okay."

He leaned closer. Even though her eyes were closed, she could feel his warm breath on her cheek. "Just breathe with me, okay? It's almost over." He inhaled and then slowly exhaled, urging her to do the same. "In." He inhaled. "And out." He exhaled. "In. And out," he chanted, rhythmically whispering in her ear. "You with me, Maya?"

"I'm with you," she whispered.

"Keep breathing. In. And out."

Maya's senses were on fire with his close proximity— his scent, his sound, the feeling of his hand and his breath on her skin, it all worked together to completely intoxicate her and keep her focus on nothing but him. "In. And out." She breathed deeply.

The sound of the seat belt sign turning off broke her out of her trance. She opened her eyes and saw his face scant inches from her own, looking at her with a strange expression. He was breathing heavily, and they remained stuck in place for a couple of seconds, and as the rest of the passengers began to relax and move about the cabin, they were forced to come back to their senses and break apart. They sat back in their own seats.

Maya took a deep breath. "Thank you for that." She laughed. "You might not have noticed but I was freaking out just a little bit."

"I didn't notice," he replied with a small laugh, not looking at her, but running a hand through his hair. "And it was no problem. I'm glad I could help. It's the least I could do for the woman who arranged for a meeting with Garrett Collins. I really do owe you much more for that."

Maya smiled. Looking into his eyes, it was easy to forget that she had been on a shaking plane, and on the verge of a panic attack. "You don't owe me anything. It's all part of my job."

11

MAYA WATCHED JAMIE pace back and forth in the living room of his suite. He was normally so calm and cool, she wasn't used to seeing him so nervous and out of sorts. He walked from one end of the room to the next, alternating between wringing his hands and raking them through his hair—a sure indication that he was nervous.

"Jamie, you'll wear a hole in the carpet if you don't stop pacing."

He stopped and looked at her as if he didn't even know that she was in the room. "Sorry," he muttered before taking off his suit jacket. He seemed to reconsider and he put it back on.

Garrett Collins was scheduled to arrive for their informal meeting in about ten minutes. Even though it would only be a casual get-together, just a friendly chat over drinks really, Jamie had explained to her that someone like Garrett Collins would be a good ally to have in the industry. And the research she had done on him had taught her much about the resort hotel magnate. In fact, he would be an extraordinary ally for herself as well, so she had helped Jamie prepare.

Maya didn't like seeing him so nervous. She admired the confident man she worked for, and even though she knew he typically carried a ton of weight on his shoulders, he never showed uneasiness like he did at the moment.

She was also nervous about the meeting. She knew that a lot was riding on the two men getting along well and the meeting being successful. But she also knew that there was no room for both of them to be a nervous wreck. So Maya had to step up. Somebody had to set Jamie Sellers straight.

"You have got to relax." She stood and walked to him. "Garrett Collins is not going to take you seriously if you're a nervous wreck."

He scowled. "Maya, listen—"

"No, you listen." She put her hands on his shoulders. "You are Jamie-goddamn-Sellers. When you talk, people listen. You are the most intelligent, confident, sure-footed man I have ever known. And Garrett Collins should be so lucky that you want to meet with him." She pushed a palm into his chest. "So pull it together, okay? This industry is all about image. You have to make us both look good here."

Jamie blinked, slightly taken aback, but Maya stood her ground, not cowering at the outburst she knew was coming. She had never spoken to him like that, and she was certain that nobody ever had in his life. He took in a deep breath.

She continued on, spurred by the confidence he lacked at the moment. "And if you're still nervous, you have to ball it up and shove it." She pointed a finger in his face, not afraid of any consequences she might face after this pep talk. "Fake it till you make it, am I right?"

Surprisingly, his lips actually twitched with amusement. "You're right," he muttered.

"Am I right, Jamie?" she asked loudly, and shook his shoulders.

"You're right!" he shouted. "I am Jamie-goddamn-Sellers," he yelled in her face, smiling while pounding one fist into his palm. "I can do this!"

Maya laughed and removed her hands from his broad shoulders. "I'm sorry I had to do that. Are you good now?"

He nodded, a broad smile on his face, amused by her way of psyching him up. "Maya, I'm great. Thank you for that. I needed it. You know, there's just a lot riding on a friendly relationship with this man." She knew that, of course, but he had not yet discussed the specifics with her. "It's nothing I'm ready to talk about quite yet, and I'm sure you realize that. But thank you. I'm glad you were here to talk me down."

"I figured it was part of the job description—shout some sense into your boss. It was one of my university courses, in fact," she teased.

"Really?" he played along. "Boss Management 101? Seems like it'd be worth the price of tuition."

Maya laughed. "It definitely was…" She trailed off, when she realized that Jamie's smile had disappeared. He was looking at her with a strange expression—one that she could now easily identify as desire. She held her breath, her heart began to thump wildly against her chest. He reached out and touched her cheek, his palm flattening against her heated skin.

He drew closer to her, and before they touched, the phone rang. He backed up and smiled at her without humor. "Saved by the phone again, right?"

Maya laughed. Not so much a laugh as the sound of air escaping her lungs. She stepped back quickly and answered the phone. "Hello, Jamie Sellers's room. Maya speaking."

The familiar voice of Andre, Garrett's assistant responded. "Hello, Maya, this is Andre, Mr. Collins's assistant. I just wanted to say, we're running a little late. Mr. Collins got held up in a meeting, and we'll be there in about fifteen minutes."

JAMIE AND MAYA spent the next four days going about the convention rigmarole. They attended workshops, lectures, presentations, and Jamie even did a presentation of his own. Which he nailed. The meeting with Garrett Collins had gone splendidly. He was absolutely charmed by Jamie, as Maya knew he would be.

When they exited the last event of the convention, they realized that they still had most of their last day left to explore the city. Maya was looking forward to the opportunity to check out some of the sights of the Las Vegas Strip on their last day, but she knew Jamie was a workaholic, so she assumed that he would have something planned to keep them busy.

Maya turned to him. "So, what's the agenda for the rest of the day?" She scrolled through the calendar on her phone and didn't see anything that they'd scheduled.

Jamie held the door for her and they stepped outside into the blazing Nevada sun. "Wow," he huffed. "I keep forgetting about the heat. Quite a departure from Montreal, hey?"

"Isn't it, though. I love it. The hotter the better," she remarked, slipping her sunglasses over her eyes. Jamie glanced at her, and he obviously did not miss the hint of unintentional innuendo in her phrasing.

"Anyway, we're free all day. But there is something I want to show you before we go hog wild," he told her.

"Sounds good. Let's do it."

Jamie called a car service and when the black Mercedes arrived, they got in. Jamie had not yet told her what he wanted to show her and she was bursting with anticipation.

"So are you going to tell me where we're going, or what?"

Jamie smiled, looking out the window. "We're almost there," he chided, with a smile. "You're so impatient."

When the car came to a stop, it was outside a recently closed property situated a little farther back from the Las Vegas Strip. At only around ten stories high, the building was much smaller than those that surrounded it. Maya got out of the car and looked up at the building. "Jamie, what is this?"

He looked at her with the excited grin of little boy on Christmas. He took her hand and walked to the front door. He pulled out a large set of keys and used one to open the front door and then led her inside. The lobby of the hotel was dusty, but in good repair and not too dated. It was as if the place hadn't been closed for very long, and furniture and fixtures were covered with sheets of plastic.

Maya looked around and then at Jamie, questions in her eyes.

Jamie also took in the place. But his excited, vibrant eyes saw promise. "Maya, this property will be the home of the first American Swerve Hotel and Nightclub," he told her with great pride and anticipation.

"Jamie, are you serious?" She took a look around, and she knew that she wasn't alone when she could envision what this old building could be, what Jamie could make of it. "Is this the big secret project you've been working on? Why you wanted to meet with Garrett Collins?"

"It is. I wanted to play it close to my chest. I didn't want to let anyone know what I was thinking in case it didn't actually happen, and you know that I can't deal with failure." He walked into the center of the lobby and pulled the plastic sheets from the furniture, covering his clothes in dust and dirt in the process. He didn't seem to mind.

"Opening locations internationally is always a tricky thing. If it didn't work out, I didn't want anyone to know that I'd failed, and damage my fragile male pride. And the meeting with Garrett, it was just to talk about my intentions, man to man. I'm in no way looking to take him over, or to be a huge competitor of a man who owns such a huge piece of Las Vegas. But I think that it is the beginning of an easy business relationship."

Maya stopped and turned to him. Now understanding why Jamie worked so hard, and for so long. She smiled. "It's always nice to have friends in high places." She looked around again, with interest, picturing what this dusty, dirty old space would become. If anyone could turn this into a beautiful, modern and profitable space, it was Jamie Sellers. "So when do you hope to start work on this?"

"Right away. I've got crews coming in tomorrow."

"Tomorrow?"

"Yup." He smiled.

"And when will this location be opening?"

Jamie hesitated only briefly, and he looked at her, as if to guage her reaction."

"November."

Maya thought for a moment, and took a look around the lobby. "That's just a month after the opening of the Montreal hotel."

Jamie nodded. "I know it sounds insane—"

"It is!"

"Opening two hotel/nightclub properties within a month of one another is a crazy endeavor, especially when they're in two different countries. It's going to be a challenge. But I know we can handle it. It's completely under control. It's going to mean a lot more work and long hours in the office for both of us. Can you handle that?"

"I can handle it," she assured him.

He carried on. "Everything has been finalized and, just like the Montreal hotel, I've got crews that will be working around the clock to make this place spectacular. Most of the work will just be cosmetic, anyway."

Maya nodded. She trusted Jamie, and she was so proud to be a part of his team. "This is going to be incredible!"

"I know. It really is. It's going to be a lot of work, but it'll be worth it." Breaking from his trance, he turned to Maya and clasped her wrists in his large, strong hands. "Maya, let's go to dinner tonight, to celebrate. To decompress. I think after the last few days, we need to let loose a little tonight. This is your first trip to Vegas, after all. We can't have you all cooped up and working all the time. Let's explore a little. Have some fun. We've earned it!"

He was silent for a couple of seconds and his eyes held

hers. Maya's heart thundered. Was he going to kiss her? Was Jamie asking her out on a date? No, of course not. Sure, they had almost had a moment in his suite a few days ago, and in their office weeks ago, and who could forget about the hot tub, but they had barely touched since. They were in one of the hottest party locations in the world. He was offering them a chance to let off steam before they returned home the next day.

"Yeah, sure, let's do it," she agreed, excited to get to spend some time with Jamie when they weren't consumed by work.

"Great!" Jamie held open the door that was opaque with the desert dust. He escorted her outside and toward the car that waited for them. "Let's head back to the hotel, and we'll meet back in the lobby, at say 7:00? I'll make dinner reservations."

"That sounds fantastic," she responded as she got back into the car. She was excited to have some fun with Jamie. However, a part of her remained apprehensive. Would she be able to control herself around him? They had already had a couple of romantic near misses. If she let her guard down, would they end up making a terrible mistake? One from which they couldn't recover? She took a deep breath. With resolve she held her head high. *We're adults. We can control our hormones for one evening, can't we?*

12

BACK IN HIS SUITE, Jamie finished up a little paperwork on his new acquisition, and he found he had a little more free time than he realized. More free time, in fact, than he'd had in a long time. It was almost as if in the past ten years he'd forgotten how to unwind. Tonight would be a good refresher. A night for him to feel like the young man he was. With no work, phone calls or emails to distract him, he and Maya would have fun. He was sure of it.

He had pulled a few strings and was able to secure reservations at a high-end steak house run by a celebrity chef, and a friend had given him tickets to a Cirque du Soleil performance for later that night. Even though he had lived in Montreal all his life, he honestly didn't know much about that type of show, but he was hoping Maya would enjoy it. She'd been working so hard for him, and he wanted to treat her to a spectacular night out, something special, before they returned to the mountain of new work that awaited them back home in Montreal.

But this wasn't a date. *Not a date.* It couldn't *be* a date, and he wouldn't *let* it be a date. This evening would just be two colleagues enjoying dinner, a show, and checking out some of the sights. That's it. Just a friendly night out… A night out with his beautiful, funny, intelligent assistant.

He shook his head, pulling his tie free from the collar of his shirt, and he walked toward the large bathroom of his suite. He started the shower—turning it to cold. He unbuttoned his shirt and pulled it free from his pants. He dropped it on the floor and let his gray pants drop in a pool at his feet. He stood at the mirror and regarded his reflection. In his eyes, he saw the strain of overwork and stress, and the crow's-feet starting to form at their corners. He sighed, and ran his hand through his hair. A habit he didn't realize he'd had until Maya pointed it out. He smiled, thinking of her, the response causing him to feel a twitch in his lower half at the memory of having her in his lap in the hot tub. He lowered his hand below his waist and took himself in hand.

Since hiring Maya, he had taken matters into his own hands, so to speak, more times and had taken more cold showers than ever in his life. He wanted her more than he could have ever imagined wanting a woman. But he had to remain…firm. He couldn't have her. And this was how his life would be. This was his only way to keep away from Maya. He knew that if he let his guard down, or succumbed to any moment of weakness, he would cave. He turned to the shower and, bracing himself, he stepped under the freezing blast of shower spray.

INSTEAD OF USING the afternoon to explore more of the sights in Las Vegas, Maya used it to treat herself to some of the hotel's spa services. First was the mani/pedi, followed by a bikini wax, a hot stone massage and an appointment to have her hair and makeup professionally applied and styled. She wanted to make sure she looked absolutely perfect tonight when Jamie saw her. *It's not like it's a date*, she told herself. She wouldn't get her hopes up that tonight would be anything more than just a fun night out as two colleagues, and at most two friends. *Two friends who felt each other up in a hot tub, you mean.*

Standing in front of the mirror in her hotel room, Maya took in her appearance and smiled. She wasn't a conceited woman, but she knew she looked good. The hair and makeup stylists had cost a fortune, but she was glad she had taken advantage of the services. This was her last night in Vegas, after all. And Maya wanted to look the part of the glamorous type of woman Jamie Sellers was no doubt accustomed to being seen with.

Opening the small hotel room closet, she sighed when she looked over the business suits and convention-appropriate clothing that she had brought. It had been an oversight on her part to not pack something more fitting for a night out on the town with Jamie. She obviously needed to buy something better. Checking her watch, she decided that she had just enough time to head to the Forum Shops at Caesars Palace. With so many luxury shops at her disposal, Maya would no doubt find what she was looking for there. And she needed an outfit that was fitting for a night out with a gorgeous man…

"I mean, my boss," she corrected herself before leaving her hotel room.

"MAYA, I'M REALLY glad I hired you." Jamie leaned away from the table and sat back in his chair. The restaurant was perfect. The food, the wine and the atmosphere were all quite spectacular, and the favor he had called in to get the reservations was well worth it. But they might as well have been eating at a McDonald's because everything that surrounded them paled in comparison to his date, *ahem*, companion, for the evening. He raised his wineglass in her direction. "You've been an amazing assistant. I don't know how I would get anything done without you."

Maya smiled and he watched her. A blush crept across her face and chest. "I'm just doing my job. Thank you for the amazing opportunity. I'm having a great time working for you. I'm learning so much."

"I'm glad. I know I can't keep you forever, but I hope I can at least help you move on to bigger and better things. Oh!" Jamie sat straighter. "I almost forgot. A friend of mine got me a couple of tickets for Cirque du Soleil tonight. I hope you enjoy that sort of thing."

Her mouth dropped. "I love Cirque du Soleil. Which show?"

Jamie put a hand inside his jacket and fished out the two tickets. "I'm not sure. I don't really know much about it." He passed the tickets over to her.

Her eyes sparkled with enthusiasm. "This is so exciting. I didn't think we'd get a chance to see a show." She accepted the tickets and then looked down at them. "Oh." She pursed her lips when she saw the name of the show.

"What? What is it?" Jamie leaned forward.

"The show. It's *Zumanity*."

"Okay...?" He shook his head. The name didn't ring any bells.

"It's the *adults only* show. 'The sensual side of Cirque.' It's supposed to be pretty erotic."

"Oh." Jamie sat back. Outwardly, he was playing it

cool. But inside, he was freaking out. *What is the matter with me? Why didn't I check out the name of the show? Idiot!* he scolded himself. How could he take the woman he'd wanted more than any other to a sexy acrobatic show? How would he control the basic urges he'd been denying this whole time? He would surely need a bucket of ice water to throw over his head during intermission.

"I'm sorry about that. We don't have to go if you don't want to. I swear. It wasn't my intention to embarrass you."

"Who's embarrassed?" Maya scoffed. "We're both adults, we can surely sit in a theater and take in a show, can't we?"

Jamie laughed uneasily, picking up the dessert menu. "Of course we can. How do you feel about dessert? I hear they have a great crème brûlée here."

MAYA AND JAMIE were silent as they exited the *Zumanity* theater. Maya thought about the show. It was a fantastic display of the feats of the human body, but there was no denying the sexual and downright erotic nature of the show.

She wasn't uncomfortable during the show, but several times she felt Jamie squirm in his seat beside her. *Is ladies' man Jamie Sellers afraid of a little sex?* She smiled secretly at the thought and quickly dismissed it. There was no way that Jamie was anything less than all man. He would be completely confident in bed and as skillful and resourceful in the bedroom as he was in the boardroom. She could tell, from their kiss, their hot tub excursion and the way he moved and spoke and briefly touched her that he would not be uncomfortable at all with the idea of sex. That he would, no doubt, take the passion that he normally devoted to his work and apply it to lovemaking and pleasing a woman. She heated at the thought.

She glanced at him out of the corner of her eye and saw him walking rigidly next to her. "So what now?" she asked brightly, attempting to break the tension. "This is my first trip. Show me how Party Animal Jamie Sellers does Vegas."

"PARTY ANIMAL?" JAMIE LAUGHED to himself. His trips to Vegas as of late had involved real estate meetings, conference calls and meeting with lawyers. He hadn't made time to socialize, or drink and gamble. "I figured we could hit a few nightclubs. See what's trending here, bring it back home."

"Jamie, do you think of anything but work?" she asked him with a laugh.

"Rarely," he admitted, without humor, looking straight ahead. He often thought about work. But at that moment, he could think of nothing but the beautiful woman next to him. He pictured the erotic acts and the sexuality demonstrated in the show, and it was all he could do to not picture himself and Maya as the acrobats. Naked bodies gyrating, rubbing against each other, stretching the limits of their flexibility. Now, on the street, he couldn't bring himself to look directly at her, lest he take her right on the sidewalk. He was so hard, he could barely walk, and he hoped against hope that she didn't glance down and notice his desire for her. A desire that for about a month now, he'd kept under strict control. Now he felt like a crazed man. An animal. Before tonight, he'd had the slimmest of grips on his self-control, and he could feel it slipping more and more out of his grasp with each passing second.

Just go back to your room. Jamie willed himself. *Just go back, take care of this yourself and take yet another cold shower and get into bed.*

Jamie chanced a quick glance at Maya and she was looking at him with a curious expression. He realized that she had been speaking to him, but he'd been so busy concentrating on not pushing her against a wall and wrapping himself up in her that he forgot that they were talking. It was embarrassing to admit he hadn't heard a word that she had said.

"Sorry? I didn't catch that."

"We aren't going to a club," she told him matter-of-factly.

"We aren't?"

"Nope. Because if we go to a club, I know that you won't relax. You'll be in work mode the entire time. Making comparisons, brainstorming."

He smiled. She was right. Maybe he was too easy to read. "You're absolutely right. So what do you suggest we do?"

"How about we hit a casino or two? See if we can win some money?"

Jamie laughed. Not that he intended to build a casino in his hotel. He had done enough research on the topic, and in all of his research of casino ownership and profit and loss margins, he knew that the probability of them winning anything was low. But he wanted Maya to have a good time, so he would do whatever it was she wanted. "Yeah, sure. Let's do that. We can't spend time in Vegas without giving most of our money back to the city, now can we?"

"Of course," she continued, laughing. "I don't know how to play any table games. Think you could teach me?"

Jamie smiled down at her. "Absolutely."

He knew that if they were gambling, the bright lights, the sirens and the general hustle and bustle of a casino would definitely distract him from Maya's soft hair, smooth skin, deep eyes… *Okay, stop it, Sellers!* he reprimanded himself with a shake, as he escorted her into the nearest casino with one hand at the small of her back.

Although even that casual touch was almost more than he could bear.

MAYA CLAPPED HER hands and squealed with delight as the lights and sirens of the slot machine activated and dispensed a small jackpot. Maya grabbed her payment slip and wiggled it in front of Jamie's face. Secretly, she was a little bummed that only a small minority of slot machines dispensed actual coins these days—she had been looking forward to hearing the *plink, plink, plink* of the quarters falling from the machine. But the little piece of paper was pretty good, too.

"I told you I had a good feeling about this machine!" She laughed, leaning into him, a broad smile on her face. "Eight hundred dollars!" The ticket showed the number, which was a lot of "free money" to her. Sure, Jamie paid her well, but swinging in Jamie's circles and being exposed to his life was quite a change of pace for her. She smiled at her winnings. But she imagined that it was most likely small potatoes to Jamie.

"That's great!" Jamie said with a smile.

"Come on!" Suddenly hit by inspiration, Maya took Jamie's arm and dragged him across the floor.

"Where are we going?"

"Drinks are on me." She turned her head to him, still pulling on his arm.

"Maya, you don't have to buy drinks. Let me—"

"No, Jamie," she insisted. "You're always buying lunch and dinner for us at the office. Let me do this."

"All right," he finally relented. "The first round is on you. Second is on me. That's my compromise."

JAMIE COULD ONLY laugh when he saw where Maya had led him as she held on to his arm and practically dragged him across the casino. Really, she didn't have to pull so hard. He was sure that he would have followed her anywhere.

"So, what is this?" he asked her, smiling broadly, as they stood in front of a frozen daiquiri bar, a common stop for tourists on the Strip.

"For five days now, I've watched everyone walking around with these, and I want one." She turned to the man behind the counter and held up two fingers and pointed to the ridiculously large, yard-long drinking receptacles. When they were poured, she passed one to Jamie. He had never had one before and he wasn't looking forward to the blast of sugar he knew was coming.

He watched Maya as she took a sip. He couldn't help but feel aroused at the way she lowered her face and closed her eyes when her lips closed over the straw. His breath caught, and he was mesmerized when her cheeks hollowed. His cock stirred, imagining how her mouth would feel wrapped around it instead of the wide straw.

Her eyes went wide as she disengaged from the drink. "Wow! That's strong!"

Curious, he took a sip and was surprised when it felt like the alcohol overtook the sugar content. He wondered if the owner of the stand knew how strong the employees were mixing the daiquiris. If that happened in his bar, he would be livid. *Let it go, man. You're not working. You're on vacation tonight.* "You're not wrong." He took another sip. *Not bad, though.*

They walked with their drinks in companionable silence. She drank some more, seeming to enjoy it more this time. "I'd better be careful." She looked him straight in the eyes, her own blazing. "We both remember what happened the last few times we had a little too much to drink," she said to him huskily.

His breath caught in his throat. She was alluding to their first meeting, when she had kissed him at his club, followed promptly by their brief hookup after the party. His head lowered slightly, not looking away from her. "Maya—" he cautioned.

She smiled and then laughed. "I'm kidding, Jamie!" she said a little too loudly. "That is all so in the past. You're my boss. It's not going to happen again," she insisted. "Don't worry."

He shook his head and took another sip of his drink. She was trying to reassure him that *she* wouldn't jump *his* bones? "That's right. It can't happen again." Jamie needed to go back to his room. He needed to get away from her before his libido gained complete control over him and he took her right there in the middle of the Strip.

He looked at his watch. "Why don't we head back to the hotel? We've had a pretty long day and we have an early flight tomorrow."

He thought he saw something flicker, just for a second, in her eyes. Disappointment? He didn't want to be the one to put that look on her face. But getting them both safely back to their rooms, fully dressed, was their only option.

"Yeah, sure." Once again her gaze turned heated. "I think it's time to get into bed."

13

So THERE THEY WERE, walking to their hotel on the Las Vegas Strip, dressed immaculately in clothes that were far too expensive, in shoes that were far too uncomfortable and finishing their absolutely ridiculous yard-long frozen daiquiris that were far too strong, desperately tiptoeing around and fighting against the sexual tension between them that was far too obvious.

Maya's legs quivered with her want for him. She covertly squeezed her thighs together in an effort to satiate the thrum at her core. It didn't work. Jamie had already made it abundantly clear that he didn't want anything to do with her, in a romantic sense. He flat out told her that their relationship could be nothing but professional from that moment on. And she had wholeheartedly agreed. She wasn't about to jeopardize her name and reputation in a close-knit industry just because she was attracted to her boss.

But a girl can't help but dream, can she? She sighed, a little too loudly because it got his attention and he looked at her, in question. She ignored his gaze. If she chanced a glance at him, it would be too much. So she stared straight ahead and continued to drink her daiquiri. The rum was starting to affect her. She felt loose, languid, aroused. *I'll have to take care of that later, too,* she surmised. She would no doubt be picturing Jamie above her as she pleasured herself later in her room.

He sighed next to her. She quickly glanced at him, as he brought his hand to his hair. He wore a scowl deeply etched on his handsome face, stubborn determination in his eyes. Was he possibly feeling the frustration and need that she was? It had never occurred to her that the want was just as hard for him to deal with.

When they arrived back at their hotel they looked out of place in the opulent lobby of the Bellagio, dressed in their exquisite clothing, holding the plastic novelty drinkware in their hands, but neither of them cared. They stood wordlessly. She was too focused on not ripping his clothes off to speak or make any sudden movements.

When the elevator opened before them, they entered, and Maya pushed the button for the twelfth floor. Jamie did nothing. He made no movement to push the button for his own floor.

When she looked at him quizzically, he responded curtly. "I'll walk you to your room."

"Okay." She nodded. "Thank you." *Don't read too much into this, Maya. He's just being a gentleman to get you to your room safely. Just don't pull him inside and ravage him.*

In the silence of the elevator, the only noise was their breathing, as they climbed higher to Maya's floor. They arrived, and the doors pulled open. Still not speaking, they exited together. Jamie placed a hand at the small of her back, escorting her into the corridor. His touch sizzled and she flinched slightly. He quickly pulled his hand away and put it back in his pocket.

As they turned the corner, Maya dug into her purse and produced her room key. "Well, this is me," she told him, stopping outside of her room. It occurred to her that Jamie had not come to her room once during this trip. He always insisted that she meet him in the lobby, or in a nearby restaurant.

"Well…" She cleared her throat, moving to unlock the door. "I guess I'll see you tomorrow morning. I'll call—" Her words were stopped in her throat when she felt Jamie grab her arm to spin her around to face him. The look on his face was animalistic, hungry. With a growl, he pushed her into the door and leaned in, his lips crashing violently against hers.

Oh God. Oh God. Oh God. She didn't imagine she would ever again have the opportunity to kiss Jamie Sellers. They had all but sworn it off. This man was outright devastating her mouth with his own. She tilted her head to allow him better access, and his lips slanted over hers, deepening the kiss, and she moaned into his mouth when he found her own tongue.

They both dropped their empty glasses on the floor, and her arms wrapped around his neck while his found her waist. They dipped lower, over her hips and down her ass.

Jamie continued his exploration of her entire body. He groaned and ground his pelvis, his hard, rigid erection, into her belly. She thought she would fall over, if not for the hard body pinning her to the door.

As quickly as he had kissed her, he broke away. "Dammit," he growled. He looked up and down the hallway, they were alone. He ran his hand through his hair and with his other hand he reached out and cupped her cheek.

At the gentle contact, Maya closed her eyes and leaned into his touch. He pulled away and took her hand, leading her back down the hallway to the elevator. "Come on."

14

"WHAT?" MAYA STUMBLED on her words and her feet. "Where are we going?"

"We're going to my room," he said, his voice gruff. He pulled her into the elevator. If he was going to take her to bed, it would be in his luxury suite like she deserved, not some normal, *typical* hotel room.

Jamie wasn't sure what had happened. But when she'd turned to go into her room, he was like a man possessed. His dick was officially in charge. He had grabbed her arm and kissed her before he could even manage to stop himself. He knew he was making a mistake and that he shouldn't take Maya back to his room. But it was too late now. He needed her like he needed air to breathe. At that moment, he didn't care about tomorrow...or the next day. They had tonight, and that was it. Consequences be damned.

Back in the elevator, he looked at her. Like himself, she was breathing heavily, staring straight ahead. The expression on her face was unreadable. *What is she thinking?* He shook his head. *I should just tell her to go back downstairs.* He should. But he wouldn't. He couldn't.

His thoughts were interrupted when the elevator door opened with a chime. They were on his floor, but neither moved to get off.

"Maya," he whispered. When she turned to him, he saw the same uncertain desire that he felt clouding her features.

Jamie was asking her. He was giving her an out. He was caught between the hope that she would either come to her senses, tell him that it wasn't going to happen, or let him rip her dress off in the elevator. "It's up to you."

Maya nodded and she paused for a moment. "Let's go."

WHEN JAMIE TOOK her hand and led her to his suite, she sighed softly. *Finally.* Finally she would once again feel those lips, those hands, on her. And this time, there would be no phone interruptions; she wouldn't pull away from him. This was going to happen. She followed him blindly until they finally arrived to double doors that led to his suite.

He dropped her hand to reach into his jacket for his key card. She noticed a slight tremble in his hand and she relaxed a little, knowing that he was as affected as she was. He opened the door and ushered her quickly inside.

She inhaled sharply when she felt Jamie come from behind her and place his large hands on her shoulders. She felt his warmth through the material of her dress, and she closed her eyes and sighed.

He moved her hair away from her neck and bent over her shoulder. He placed his lips on the sensitive flesh where her neck met her shoulder, and she shuddered. "Jamie," she whispered, and then hissed when his tongue traced a line on her flesh, across her shoulder until it met her dress. With an impatient groan, he turned her around so she faced him.

"Maya," he murmured, his hands running down her ribs to rest low on her hips. "I want you so badly."

She nodded and opened her mouth. She could barely form words. "I—I want you, too, Jamie."

"Thank God." His voice was low and he bent slightly and touched his lips to hers. Tentatively, at first. But when Maya parted her lips, his tongue surged forward and sought out hers. She placed her palms flat on his chest. Even through his shirt and jacket, she could make out the hardness of his chest. Her hands traveled south, to run over the firm bumps of his abdominal muscles. Before she reached the zipper of his pants, he took both of her wrists in the grasp of one large hand.

"Not yet." He took her mouth once more, and it was his turn to run his hands over her dress. From her hips, he reached behind and grabbed her ass and squeezed. She moaned into his mouth and he continued his exploration. He brought his palms to the bodice of her dress and reached around her back and pulled down her zipper.

She felt the dress loosen around her chest and shoulders. He continued to kiss her, as each tooth in the long zipper unhinged, one by one. He clouded every one of her senses. He was all she could see, hear, feel, smell, taste. He was everywhere around her.

Jamie pushed the straps from her shoulders and let the dress fall to her feet. He stepped back so he could see her body, clad only in her bra and panties, made from a thin, filmy lace, which didn't leave much to the imagination, and her black stilettos, with the red soles, for which she'd spent far too much money. Worth it. He looked her up and down. A wolfish smile playing on his lips and hunger in his eyes. "You're perfect."

Perfect. Jamie Sellers said she was perfect. She moved her hands to her sides and stood tall, silent. Unfortunately, he was still plenty dressed.

"Let's get rid of your clothes now. Shall we?" She put her hands on his shoulders and pushed his expensive gray jacket from his broad shoulders.

When it hit the floor, it seemed as if something in him snapped. He lifted her, and she wrapped her legs around his waist, and he made his way down the hallway to the bedroom.

JAMIE STRODE INTO the room and deposited her gently on the fluffy white duvet on the king-size bed, and she leaned against the mountain of pillows, and she watched, with her clever eyes, as he walked across the room to a toiletry bag he kept on the dresser. He removed a handful of foil-wrapped condoms and deliberately put them on the nightstand.

He looked down at the woman on his bed. His assistant, his friend, the woman he had lusted over for more than a month, the woman he had vowed to himself that he would never have. Maya was lying on his bed in her barely there lingerie and those incredible shoes.

He started unbuttoning his shirt. And with every movement, he could feel his cock grinding against the zipper of his pants. He had never been so hard, or needed a woman as much as he needed her. He'd ignored this need, this obviously mutual attraction, for too long. *This feels right.* Being with Maya felt as natural as breathing, and he knew that he would have to have her again…and again…and again.

He pulled his shirt free from the waist of his pants and threw it to the floor, he unzipped his pants and allowed them to follow suit. He chuckled when her eyes locked on his midsection and his near-painful erection, as it was straining the elastic of his boxer briefs.

He kept the shorts on and kneeled on the bed, slowly making his way to her. He leaned over her, kissing her. She tasted so sweet, like the sugary rum of their drink, which remained on her tongue. He didn't think he would ever get enough of kissing her.

When he reached her bent knees, Jamie placed a palm on both and spread them slowly. He was captivated by the look of her. They locked eyes and he moved closer. Taking her mouth in another tender, but demanding kiss. Her long legs wrapped around his waist, and he felt the stiletto heels dig into his lower back. He grimaced at the sharp pain, but he didn't care. It was only a miniscule pain compared to the ache he felt in his dick.

Maya moaned when he pressed his engorged erection against her center, and it fueled him. Reaching behind her to unsnap her bra, he freed her breasts. They fell into his hands and he squeezed them. He lowered his face and feasted on one, then the other. He took them greedily, making up for the time in the hot tub when she'd pulled away from him. She wasn't pulling away tonight. She moaned and held the back of his head and pressed it into her chest.

"Jamie," she whimpered, as he pulled a nipple between his teeth.

He reluctantly released her breasts and began licking a trail down her middle. He passed her tight abdomen, dipped his tongue inside her navel and soon kissed his way to the neat triangle of hair of her bikini area as he tugged her panties off.

He brought his lips to her center and kissed her gently. Using his lips and his fingers, he parted her and swept his tongue up the middle until he reached the bundle of nerves at the top.

MAYA CRIED OUT in pleasure, and she clutched the hair at the back of his head and simultaneously pulled him closer and pushed him away. She was frenzied. Set adrift in a sea of Jamie. His touch, his scent, his sounds surrounded her as he brought her to climax. "Jamie, now. Please."

When he ignored her, she scraped her nails across his shoulder in a sweet protest. He hissed at the brief pain and raised his head, looking at her with a question in his eyes.

"I need you. Now," she sighed.

He chuckled against her skin, and placed a light, but firm bite on her thigh. It sent ripples across her entire body. He was so in tune with everything she needed, and he moved up her body until he lay over her, covering her, supporting his weight with his forearms and knees.

He kissed her sweetly. "All right. No more waiting." She felt his words meant more than he had probably intended to convey. Was he talking about their weeks of playing off each other, their close quarters and the palpable sexual tension that tormented them on a daily basis? Or did he just mean tonight? She wouldn't have to wait for him to make love to her?

Maya then realized that she couldn't have cared less what he meant as she watched Jamie reach for a condom. Once he was ready, he returned to her, holding himself aloft at her entrance, and with one firm thrust, he was inside of her. She gasped at the feeling of him filling her entirely.

"Maya," he whispered in her ear, before he began thrusting. Her own moans were drowned out by his, and soon waves of pleasure began to crash over her. Rising, rising, until they crested into another bone-shattering orgasm. Jamie gritted his teeth, staying with her until her pleasure had subsided and then took his own.

His comfortable weight settled over her. They were silent for a moment before Maya exhaled. "My God."

Jamie chuckled and rolled away from her, onto his back. "Yeah." He left the bed for a moment to dispose of the condom in a nearby trash can. He rolled back to her with a deep, low, satisfied sigh.

They both remained on their backs. Not speaking. Maya looked over at him and wondered if, now that it was over, Jamie had regretted making love to her. Had they crossed a line?

Suddenly feeling awkward, she turned to get off the bed. She realized that she was still wearing her shoes and they had tangled in the bedcovers. *Heaven forbid I should be able to display a little grace, here?* "Uh, I should go."

He turned to her, brow furrowed. "Why?"

"Because, what just happened. I don't think—"

Jamie reached over and touched her cheek. "Maya, stop. Us sleeping together won't be a problem unless we let it be one. And what happened here tonight doesn't have to follow us back home and into the office."

She took a deep breath. Relieved that it wouldn't put a strain on their working relationship, but also crestfallen that this wouldn't go anywhere beyond this one night.

"We're both adults," he continued. "And I think we both needed to finally get that out of our systems before we imploded. Don't you think?"

"Yes, I do think." She had spent too many waking, and sleeping, hours lusting over this man. Her boss. They needed to get all of the feelings of arousal and desire out of their systems. Now they were free to carry on and work together in a professional manner, without all of the strain they had been under.

"And it's just one night." He looked at her, desire burning once again in his eyes. Her gaze trailed lower, to his cock, already once again hard. "But tonight isn't quite over yet," he said, before grabbing her waist and pulling her astride him. "Not for a few hours yet, anyway."

15

JAMIE LOOKED UP at Maya, and in response to his sultry gaze, she swiveled her hips, grinding her center into his still-hard cock. He moaned with the sensation.

"What do you have in mind?" she asked him, scraping her fingernails down his chest. His muscles tensed under her touch.

In one swift movement he locked an arm around her waist, flipped her onto her back and he was on top of her as she squealed in surprise. He could have taken her again, but he didn't. He wanted to savor her, spend the entire night learning her body, the taste of her soft skin, her most sensitive spots, her moans and the way she laughed and whispered his name. In spite of how urgent she made him feel, he wasn't a complete animal. He wanted the night to last.

"I have an idea." He got up from the bed and walked, still nude, into the bathroom. He was once again glad that Mary had booked him a suite for his stay. It proved invaluable for his meeting with Garrett Collins, but the sheer opulence was a nice treat. Plus, it gave his night with Maya an element of fantasy, as if it wasn't actually happening in their real, everyday lives. This night was special. One that they probably wouldn't get to relive. They might as well make the most of it while they could.

Jamie turned on the water in the large marble bathtub. He didn't hear her come into the bathroom behind him.

"Well, this is certainly nicer than the bathroom in my room."

"It's not bad." Jamie shrugged casually. Then he laughed. He wasn't so much of a snob that he couldn't appreciate the finer things. He was certainly a long way from where he'd grown up. He was appreciative of every luxury that he enjoyed in his adult life, because he'd worked hard for them, and he knew how quickly they could all be taken away. "How about a bath?"

"That'd be great." She eyed the tub lustfully. "What will you do in the meantime? I think there's a hockey game on."

His mouth dropped in shock and she laughed. "Jamie, I'm obviously kidding. Won't you join me in this bathtub that was obviously built for five people?"

"Nice of you to ask. Would you mind checking the cabinet there for some bubble bath?"

"I'd love to."

Jamie watched her turn away from him and open the cabinet door. Her naked body was long and lean. Her skin an expanse of smooth, olive-colored velvet. She had tied her hair up in a loose knot and his eyes trailed from her delicate neck to her—*Wait! What is that?*

"Maya, is that a tattoo?" His eyes focused on the small butterfly low on her back, above her right hip. He must have missed it before, but now his eyes were riveted.

"Oh, yeah." She laughed, handing him a bottle of vanilla bubble bath. "That's a souvenir from freshman year. I had just moved out of my parents' house. When I was growing up they were so strict, and they always put so much pressure on me with my schoolwork and my activities. So when I finally moved out, the thrill of the freedom had me feeling wild and rebellious, and this was the result. Abby's got one, too."

Jamie poured out the bubble bath and he sat on the edge of the tub, waiting for it to fill. When Maya joined him, he took her hand. "So what happened to the rebellious Maya?"

"She almost flunked out first semester. Abby and I went out a lot, got drunk, went to parties, *experimented*." Jamie's eyebrows rose at the inflection on the word *experiment*. She laughed and shoved him playfully. "Anyway, that's when I decided I had to buckle down, hit the books and be serious."

So that's what happened. Why she was such a perfectionist. Why she worked so hard. Why she wanted to be the best. He trailed his fingers through the water. "How hot do you like it?" he asked her, an eyebrow wagging suggestively.

Her response was quick. "The hotter, the better."

Jamie chuckled and turned off the water, stood and extended his hand. "After you."

"Thank you." She stepped in first and closed her eyes when she found herself knee-deep in the large tub. She settled in and gave a contented sigh.

"That good?" Jamie watched her with interest.

"Oh, yeah," she sighed, her eyes still closed. "Join me?"

"You don't need to ask me twice." He turned and settled in the water as well, behind her, hugging her back into his chest. The hot water encapsulating his body felt incredible, but it couldn't compare to the woman he held to his chest. "That is pretty good," he murmured. "I should take baths more often."

Maya wiggled a little in her spot between his thighs, as she settled in. "I love baths. It's the only way I know how to relax."

Jamie smoothed his hands over her flat tummy. "Really? The only way?" He looped one of his legs around hers, the action spreading hers with ease. His hand slid deeper into the water, until he reached her warm center. He dipped his fingers inside her warmth, and she moaned and brought her head back to rest on his chest.

While his right hand played below the water, the fingers of his left danced lightly over her neck and chest, then dropped to graze her breasts. Her nipples were stiff with anticipation and need. Jamie brushed past one with the palm of his hand and she stiffened in his arms. Dropping his head to her shoulder, he dipped his lips to the hollow of her shoulder while he plucked and played with the most sensitive parts of her body.

Maya gasped and thrashed lightly in his arms. While water splashed onto the marble tiles of the floor, the realization hit him, as if he hadn't thought of it before. He and Maya were together. She was his, if only for one night. Her naked body pressed against his, as his cock flexed against her back. His fingers brought her to a shattering climax, as she cried out and shuddered in his arms.

As she calmed, he pressed his lips to the top of her head and wrapped his arms around her. He moved from behind her and got out of the tub. He reached for the large Egyptian-cotton towels and wrapped one around his waist. He extended his hand and helped her stand. His breath hitched at the sight of the water cascading down her dark skin in long rivulets. He wrapped the other towel around her shoulders and scrubbed her lightly, drying her, as he pulled her into a scorching kiss that transmitted every need he had.

He scooped her up in his arms and brought her back to the bedroom. He knew it was late, but he didn't care. If this one night was all they would have, he would certainly take everything he could get.

16

MAYA WOKE UP with the sun in her eyes. *Why didn't I close the curtains before turning in?* She squinted her eyes against the sunlight to look past it out the window, which was now somehow larger than she remembered. It was a sliding glass door. *My room doesn't have a balcony.* She bolted upright, clutching the duvet to her chest. She looked down at the bed and saw Jamie stirring from his own sleep beside her.

"Maya?" he asked, his voice hoarse from sleep. "Everything okay?"

Okay? He wants to know if everything is okay? In the harsh light of morning, Maya reflected on what they had done the night before. His hands and lips passing every surface of her body, scorching trails that she was certain would still be visible. He'd made her cry out, whimper and tremble beneath and on top of him. *And he wants to know if everything is okay?*

Maya wasn't okay. She'd had earth-shattering, mind-blowing, benchmark-setting sex with Jamie, a man that literally held her future career and reputation in his hands. A man she told herself would stay off-limits to her. She looked around for her purse. Her clothes. Anything. "What time is it?" she demanded, not finding any of her belongings.

Last night, she had been crazed. Hormonal. They were celebrating a successful business trip. She'd had that superboozy daiquiri. She promised herself that she would never, *ever*, drink again. She scolded herself. *You clearly can't be trusted when you're drinking, Maya.* She searched for any and every excuse to explain how she ended up in Jamie's bed.

Jamie removed his shirt, which he had carelessly thrown over the bedside clock. "Ten minutes to seven."

"Oh, God." She brought her hands to her head. "I didn't mean to fall asleep here."

"Maya, it's fine," he said, his voice level.

"No, it's not. I've got to get out of here," she told him, still clutching the sheet to her breasts. "There are enough people from the convention staying at this hotel that if someone notices me leaving your suite, in last night's clothes, people are going to assume, *correctly*, that I spent the night with you."

"Okay, you're right," he reasoned.

"Where are my clothes?"

Jamie glanced around the room. "Your dress is over by the door."

Maya measured the distance between the bed and the door, and wondered how to go about keeping the sheet that was covering her. "Can you look away?"

He was incredulous. "Are you serious?"

"Yes. Please look away. I need to get my dress."

"Maya, we were pretty intimate, in several different ways last night, and we were naked the whole time." He started listing out the things that they had done to, for and with each other only hours ago. His voice a low murmur that echoed through Maya's core, and under the sheet, he ran a hand slowly up her thigh. "So, Maya, I don't think it really matters if I see you naked one more time, does it?"

Maya glared at Jamie. He was still gorgeous, and sexy and with his hand making its way to her sweetest spot, she was at serious risk of staying in his bed with him. "Jamie," she said in a stern tone. She felt the loss of his touch, and was struck with an immediate pang of regret.

"Fine," he sighed with obvious frustration, pushing the covers away from his own body. Without an ounce of shame or regret, he strode naked to the door. His body stopped the breath in her throat as he picked her dress up from the floor. "Here." He passed it to her, and, still nude, he walked out of the room into the hotel suite, leaving her alone to get dressed.

JAMIE WAS SEATED at the table, drinking a cup of coffee, when Maya emerged from the bedroom, fully dressed in last night's clothes. When he left the room, he wasn't about to admit that her outburst had hurt his feelings. But she was right. She shouldn't be seen leaving his room. It was irresponsible for them to have fallen asleep. After the first time, hell, before they even got that far, he should have got dressed and walked her to her room. But he'd gotten greedy.

He didn't have to look at her to know that she was still stunning this morning. Her outfit and shoes were exactly what she was wearing the night before. But now, as he forced his gaze to her, he saw her mussed hair and the rosy glow and slight abrasions on her neck and collarbone, where the rough hair of his face had scraped her, the small love bites he'd left with his lips and teeth. All indications were that she had been thoroughly taken the night before. And him sitting there naked, taking her in fully dressed, he felt the slight stirring in his cock. He needed her again. The hours he had spent with her the previous night had not been enough. Not by a long shot.

He returned to his coffee, not risking looking at her for any longer. "I found your purse," he told her, gesturing to the bag in front of him on the table.

"Thanks." She walked toward him.

"Want some coffee?"

"No, thank you," she sighed quietly. She sat at the table next to him. "We need to talk."

He turned to her. "We do." They had an incredible night. But he knew that's all it could be. One night of passion. In an effort to rid them both of the sexual tension, so they could actually focus on their work. The next few months would be make or break for J. Sellers Holdings. With the expansion to include the hotel properties in Montreal and the American acquisition, Jamie needed to concentrate on his work. A lot was riding on him, and he needed to put Maya out of his thoughts.

Maya hesitated. "I'm sorry I freaked out. It wasn't fair. Last night was amazing." He opened his mouth to speak, but she held up a hand to stop him. "Let me finish, please," she pleaded. "But my career is just too important to me. I can't have people thinking that you hired me because I slept with you, or that any promotion or recommendation that might come from you have those reasons behind them. And I certainly don't want to have to question my own integrity or success."

Jamie nodded. "I can understand that," he replied. "But, Maya, I have to tell you. You are an amazing assistant. And I know that you are destined for bigger and better things. I can tell you that anything you do, and anywhere you end up, it will be because of you, and it won't be dependent on you sleeping with me or anyone else." He suddenly regretted not stopping to put on his pants, as he sat there naked with Maya, having a conversation about appropriate work relationships.

"What happened last night won't affect our working relationship. I promise. Last night was great." *Better than that, really.* "But it won't happen again. We both have to keep our eyes on the prize in the months ahead. These upcoming projects will need both of our full, undivided attention."

"I agree."

"And I know that I wasn't alone in feeling the sexual tension that's been between us the past couple of weeks."

"No, you weren't."

"So really, last night was just us getting it out of our system. We'd been drinking. We're in a strange city. So, it was almost obvious that we would end up in bed together."

"That's true," she agreed. "It couldn't be helped, really." He was relieved when a small smile played on her lips. She checked the time on her cell phone. "So I'd better go. It looks like I've got quite a few emails here that need replies."

"What time will the car be picking us up to go to the airport?"

She was at the door when she stopped. "Eleven."

Feeling that their professional relationship had been saved, he nodded and smiled. "I'll meet you in the lobby."

"Sounds good." She smiled as well and let herself out of his room.

17

THAT NIGHT, WHEN Maya entered her apartment, Abby was in the kitchen cooking a late dinner. "Maya!" she squealed, running to the door and enveloping Maya in a strong hug. "I missed you! How was your trip?"

Maya bit back a yawn. "It was really great." She was exhausted from spending the previous night with Jamie, traveling and the time difference. She yawned, longing for her own bed. But she knew that Abby would surely keep her up for at least long enough to catch up. "We met with a bunch of very important people, and I sat in on some pretty interesting workshops—"

"And how was Jamie?"

Maya stopped, feeling the color fill her cheeks. "What do you mean?"

Abby regarded her carefully, her piercing eyes narrowed. "I meant 'how was Jamie' in a general sense." Still looking strangely at Maya, she went on. "Like, how was it being with him 24/7? How did his meetings go? Did you guys get along?"

"Oh. Yeah. It was fine," Maya stammered, moving past Abby to come farther into the apartment. "How was your week? How's the job hunt going?" She hoped to distract her friend long enough so she could sneak to her bedroom and avoid the topic of Jamie altogether.

Abby was silent for a moment, before she followed Maya to her bedroom. "Pretty good. I've got some interviews lined up next week." She stopped at the entrance to Maya's room and crossed her arms across her chest as she leaned on the doorjamb, tilting her head to the side as she regarded her friend. "Maya, did you and Jamie have sex?"

Shocked, Maya's mouth dropped open. "What?" And then she sighed, too exhausted to keep up the pretense. She never could lie to her best friend. "How did you know?"

"You've got this freshly sexed look about you. I'd know it anywhere. I can basically feel it coming off you. It's like an aura." Abby curled up on Maya's bed and hugged one of her pillows. "So, how was it?"

Maya slumped down on her bed with a sigh. "It was incredible…" She trailed off for a moment to reflect on her night with Jamie, before grimacing at her reaction to him that morning. "But this morning I woke up in his bed and I freaked out." She detailed her exchange with Jamie, beginning with not wanting to dress in front of him and ending with their completely uneventful, near-silent plane ride back home. Jamie had transitioned easily back into the role of her boss, as if he hadn't sat naked at the table and offered her coffee just hours before. Had he been so unaffected that it didn't even matter? That any desire he had felt for her had been completely purged from his system?

Maya continued. "And I'm not sure why I'm so upset about it. Am I upset because it was so casual to him that he just became my boss again? Or am I upset that I know it can never happen again?" She lay back on her bed. "This was supposed to be a one night thing, to get it out of our systems. But, I feel like I want him even more now." She threw an arm over her eyes. "My God, how am I supposed to share an office with him, eat with him, travel with him, when I know so much about him now?" How his body, all firm muscle, looked beneath his suit. How his lips and warm, demanding hands felt all over her body. The look in his eyes, and his hoarse shouts when he came. How peacefully he slept beside her, before she jostled him awake, of course.

"What am I going to do?" she pleaded with her friend.

Abby rolled over to Maya and wrapped her arms around her, pulling her into a friendly, supportive hug. How many times had their current roles been reversed? When Abby had come home, devastated about some guy, and Maya had provided the comfort. "Well, hon, you have two options," she told her, in a soothing voice. "You can forget it ever happened, how he made you feel all a-tingle. You can go about your business and just focus on work."

"What's the other option?"

"You can make it impossible for him to forget it happened, and what a complete smoke show you are in bed. And make it impossible for him to think about anything but you."

Maya laughed. "I can't do that to him. This is too important a time to throw him off his game. We can't afford any distractions."

Abby gave her a parting squeeze. "Well, the last time I saw the man up close I was painfully hungover and he was still one of the best-looking guys I've ever seen, so good luck with option one."

JAMIE SAT ON his couch. He had not long arrived home. But instead of heading to his bedroom to unpack his bag, or to the kitchen to fix dinner, he dropped his bag at the door and headed straight for his liquor cabinet. He grabbed a very expensive bottle of scotch and a glass and slumped down in his living room.

What was I thinking? He shook his head in disgust. *I wasn't thinking, obviously. If I'd been thinking, I wouldn't have gone to bed with my assistant.* In his effort to be taken seriously as a businessman, Jamie had been so good and on his best behavior the past couple of years. Not giving anyone—naysayers, competitors, bloggers—anything negative to write about. It had been going so well. Until he met Maya, that is.

He put a hand to his stomach, where the scotch burned his insides. The scotch? Or was it Maya? It had been near impossible for him to not touch her during their five-hour flight. He had resorted to pretending to be asleep. All the while, he was aware of every move she made. When she ordered tea, when she got up to go to the lavatory, when she sighed in disappointment at every selection on the in-flight entertainment system.

Her reaction to waking up in his bed had shocked him. It had *hurt* him. While they were making love, he'd had a revelation. He knew that he wanted to be with Maya. He wanted to forge a relationship with her. And that morning, he had been prepared to tell her that he wanted more. He had been prepared to put himself out there and put his feelings on the line. He felt that they had formed a real connection in the early hours of the morning. And he wanted her more and more as each minute passed.

How am I going to get through this? How would he be able to focus on the important work they had coming up? If his next few steps were not successful, he could be ruined, as everything was riding on the success of the expansion. He had work to do. And he definitely couldn't be distracted by mooning over a woman. Especially not the most beautiful, dynamic, sensitive and giving lover he'd ever had.

Jamie took another swallow of the scotch, and its smooth heat enveloped him like her touch, and it triggered memories of being with her. He could feel himself start to harden. *So it's come to this again, has it?* He sighed roughly and closed his eyes, resigning himself to spend a lifetime taking cold showers.

18

FOR WEEKS AFTER returning from Las Vegas, Jamie and Maya worked tirelessly, day in and day out. Because Jamie was such a control freak, he liked to keep his work close to him. Sure, he could have hired out the hotel construction projects, but he didn't want to do that, so he and Maya shouldered most of the load of the projects.

They were busy first off, arranging contractors both in Montreal and in Las Vegas to begin working on building hotels in both locations. Sure, Jamie reckoned, it was very risky to start such huge projects at the same time, in different countries, but he was anxious to get it underway. If there was anything he loved, it was the challenge, the time crunch and fitting as much work into a weekday that he could. The time difference between Quebec and Nevada ensured that he often stayed at the office until midnight most days.

Jamie looked across the office and found Maya at her own desk. He admired Maya's need to mirror his own unhealthy work ethic. She was eager to impress. Many assistants would have definitely called it a day by 6 p.m. But not Maya. He looked at his watch as the time approached ten thirty. He watched her type furiously on her computer. In between words, she would take gulps from her coffee cup. *She must be exhausted.* He'd already suggested she go home, but she had refused. As long as Jamie was in the office, she would be, as well.

She brushed her long hair from her shoulders and used a pen to secure it in an updo, which revealed the delicate lines of her neck and throat. It had been weeks since they'd slept together. While they hadn't let themselves get too close to one another, the energy that crackled between them constantly had considerably ramped up since that night. Sometimes all it took was the sound of her voice, or a whiff of her perfume or the way she stretched at her desk to turn him on completely.

And then her clothes were another issue. While they were conservative in nature, they also fueled his dirtiest thoughts. The slim fit of her skirts and blouses only worked to highlight the exquisite body that he knew lay beneath. From time to time, *actually all the time*, his mind would stray to that night in Vegas. He pictured the lean muscles of her arms, stomach and legs. He could still feel her heat and smooth, flawless skin below him. Involuntarily, he cleared his throat to keep from moaning.

The noise caught her attention, and she looked up from her laptop and at him. "Everything okay?"

"Yeah. Everything's fine." That small break from work to think about Maya had reminded him of another of his basic needs. "Are you hungry?"

She paused, as if realizing as well that she was. "Yeah, I could definitely eat."

"Mary's gone. But we can order in. What would you like?"

She took another sip of her coffee. "It doesn't matter. I'm pretty easy."

They both caught the meaning behind her words. He cleared his throat again. "Pizza?"

"That sounds great."

"No pineapple?" he asked her, recalling her usual pizza request.

"You got it." She smiled at him as he picked up the phone to call for delivery.

A KNOCK CAME on the door a short time later. Both Jamie and Maya were still at their desks, working, and Trevor walked in holding the pizza that had been dropped off downstairs.

"I should have assumed that you were both still up here," he remarked, putting the pizza down on a coffee table. He held up a six-pack of beer—a Belgian wheat beer that Maya had grown to love. "And I brought this up from downstairs. I figured after all of the hours you've both punched this week, you guys would need to unwind a little," he finished with a wink.

Maya watched as a strange look passed between Jamie and Trevor. She had trouble determining if the good-natured look was full of meaning, or just a friendly way to sign off as Trevor left the room. *Does he know? Did Jamie tell him?* She was almost offended, but then she realized that she had told Abby immediately when she'd arrived home. Maya tried to put what had happened between them out of her mind. After seeing the amount of work that lay before them, she should have easily forgotten about making love with Jamie. "Who has time for that?" she had asked Abby earlier. So, she had intentionally left her makeup and hair understated. And she had

worn her most conservative outfits. Knee-length pen-
cil skirts, long-sleeved blouses, jackets. All in an effort
to not distract or entice the man she wanted more than
anything. She would wait him out. If they were meant
to be together, it would happen. If not, that was okay,
too. Or it would be okay. *Once I get past the crushing
heartache*, she told herself.

Trevor walked out without another word, leaving
Maya and Jamie alone with the pizza and beer, all of
which made her mouth water. She stood and straightened her skirt. She opened the pizza box, removed a
slice and put it on a paper plate Trevor had also brought
up for them. She took a bite and savored the taste, realizing that she hadn't eaten anything else since a muf-
fin she'd grabbed on the way to work that morning. She
was ravenously hungry and quickly took another bite
and then another.

She looked over at Jamie. "You better get over here
and get some of this before I eat it all."

Jamie laughed and pushed himself up from his desk.
He stopped at the beer and snagged one each for both
of them. He twisted the top off the bottle and passed it
to her. She raised an eyebrow at his implicit suggestion
that they drink while working. "Trevor's right," he told
her. "We've earned it."

"Thank you." She accepted it, and drank greedily to
wash down the mouthful of pizza. "Mmm, so good."

Realizing that there was nowhere to sit but on the
couch with her, he dropped down next to her and helped
himself to a slice. "Thanks for everything, Maya. You're
an incredible assistant. And I know that I wouldn't be
able to do all of this without you in my corner."

She flushed under his praise. It was incredible to hear

those words. She was the lucky one to have scored such a great position with such an influential man in so short a time. "You know, if you weren't such a microman-ager, we could probably get home at a decent hour," she teased him.

"But it's much more fun this way, isn't it?" he joked. "And I really appreciate you staying so late with me every night. Not everyone would do that."

"Jamie, your success is my success. And I'm really proud to be a member of your team." She held her bottle to his. "To Swerve Hotels and Nightclubs."

Jamie smiled and clinked his bottle to hers. "To hard work paying off."

It was after one in the morning when Jamie and Maya finally called it quits. They had finished the pizza and beer and got back to work. Jamie stifled a yawn and es-corted her out the front door. He was going to walk her toward her car, but realized that his was the only one in the lot. "How are you getting home?"

She turned to face him. "I'm just going to walk. It isn't far and I don't have a car and the buses don't run this late."

Jamie's mind raced. *She's walking? No way is she walking home.* "Don't be ridiculous. That's so danger-ous." He put a hand on her elbow and turned her slightly in the direction of his car. "You aren't walking. I'm driv-ing you home."

She opened her mouth to argue but he waved her off. "Don't argue. I'm not letting you walk home alone in the middle of the night."

"All right, then." She got in his car and gave him the

directions to the not-so-great neighborhood where her apartment building was located.

As he sat next to her in his car, Jamie was completely aware of her. He was exhausted, and he felt his resolve crumbling. He wanted this woman again. He'd never stopped wanting her. His hands shook with the need. He gripped the wheel tighter and looked straight ahead. But first, he needed to get her home safely.

When he parked outside her building, she was staring out the windshield. She hesitated before she turned her head and cast a look in his direction that told him that she wasn't ready to get out of the car. But when she looked away from him and muttered a quick goodbye, she reached for the door handle. With one foot outside of the car, she turned back to him.

"Jamie," she whispered, putting a hand on his arm, reminiscent of the night he had touched her as she tried to enter her hotel room in Vegas.

"What?" he asked her, his breath hushed in the small confines of his car.

In response, Maya sat back in her seat and pulled the door closed. She leaned over the console, and with a firm hand on the back of his head, she moved toward him and kissed him deeply. It was as if every emotion, every desire from the past few weeks since Vegas, had come tumbling out.

Jamie helped her over the console, while she yanked up her skirt so she could sit astride his lap, sandwiched between the hard planes of his chest and the steering wheel.

His hands ran up her thighs and she whimpered. A sound that fueled him and urged him to go further. His tongue found the sensitive spot he had previously discovered on her neck and she cried out, reaching for the buttons of his shirt. But when she got impatient, she tore at the buttons, ripping the shirt, and soon her cool hands were on his heated skin. He forced her skirt higher up her hips and ground his pelvis against her, letting her know exactly how much he needed her.

She writhed above him, telling him that her need was just as great. She reached down and ran her fingers over his hard length, before tackling his zipper.

"Oh, God," he breathed into her hair. The feeling of her fingers on him was almost too much for him. He reached into the backseat for his shoulder bag. He always kept a condom or two stashed in there. Not that he used them often. But a man had to be prepared. Blindly, and thankfully without much struggle, he reached in and located one.

In a matter of seconds, she had pulled his erection free from his boxers, and he rolled a condom over it. He slipped her panties to the side and he was inside her. Liquid heat surrounded him. Nothing had ever felt this good. Not since the last time he'd made love to her. Until this moment, he never dreamed that he would ever get a chance to be with her again. What a fool he'd been. How could he deny himself the sweet pleasure of being buried deep inside of her?

She was still. His eyes captured hers for a moment, and both sat silent, not moving. He looked into her eyes and saw wonder. He felt it, too. After what felt like an eternity she began to move above him, her hips sliding up and down, over him, sheathing him with her body. She grasped his shoulders; he could feel the pressure of her manicured nails even through his jacket.

Jamie moaned. When he began to move his hips in

time with hers, he knew he wouldn't last long. He had one hand at the small of her back, and in a moment of inspiration, he brought his thumb to her lips and slipped it inside her lush mouth. He allowed her to suckle it and swirl her tongue around it for a moment until he removed it, brought it to the little knot of nerves at her center. At the smallest touch, he felt her tense around him. He knew she was close. He circled her clit with his thumb until he felt her contract around him, and she cried out loudly in the closed confines of her car. Finally, he felt himself push over the edge. With a hoarse shout of his own, he came.

The windows had long since fogged up, but neither had noticed. Jamie could only see and feel Maya above him. The air from his lungs puffed out loudly and he breathed in the intoxicating scent of her hair. The smell mixed with the smells of sweat, sex and unadulterated lust. He focused only on breathing her in.

Maya was the first to come to her senses, and she carefully disengaged from her position straddling Jamie's lap. Moving gingerly away from the steering column, most likely bruised and something she would definitely be feeling for the next few days, she came to rest in the passenger's seat.

With a sweet smile that just about made him melt, she looked over at him. "Would you like to come up for some coffee or something?"

It was almost 2 a.m. and he knew that neither of them would be drinking coffee. But there was no way he would refuse an invitation like that. "Yeah." He smiled back. "I'd like that."

"We have to be quiet. Abby's home," Maya whispered, leading him into her apartment.

"I think we can manage that," he whispered back, his lips pressing into her hair.

When they got to her apartment, she walked to the kitchen and paused. "I don't really want coffee. It's like two in the morning. That would just be silly, wouldn't it?"

Jamie feigned shock and put a hand to his heart. "Did you use coffee to lure me into your apartment under false pretenses?" He snickered.

"Kind of. Do you want to go to my bedroom?"

"I would like that very much."

She extended her hand, and he took it, and she led him into her bedroom. Maya prayed that she remembered to tidy up before she left for work that morning. She hoped that there weren't any bras or undies left on her floor, or empty Doritos bags on her dresser. Her small bedroom, while never actually dirty or too messy, was generally quite cluttered. She blamed it on the lack of space, but in reality she often let it get messy. She'd spent so much of her childhood trying to be perfect for her parents that not cleaning her room was her small form of rebellion. She was often most comfortable when it was untidy.

When she opened the door, she said a silent prayer in thanks that her room was mostly clean. She turned to him. "Sorry it's so small. Probably smaller than you're used to."

He cast an appraising look around and smiled. "It's fine. It's great."

Suddenly her space seemed way too small. Jamie's huge frame seemed to take up the entire room and she noticed the temperature had risen at least twelve-hundred degrees since they'd entered. She could smell his cologne and wondered if, hoped that, the intoxicating scent would seep into everything she owned.

He interacted with the things in her most private space. He looked around. He touched the spines of the books on her shelves. He smoothed his hand over her dresser, grazing her hairbrush. He picked up a stuffed moose that she had picked up at a gas station while on a road trip with Abby.

"His name is Mr. Moose Ba-Goose," she explained.

He held it up to his face and laughed. How could a laugh suck all of the life-giving oxygen out of her room? "He's cute."

"Thanks. Listen, Jamie, there is a reason I invited you up here."

"Oh?" Jamie put her moose down and turned to her. "I assumed that you were hoping to take advantage of my hot body," he joked.

She smiled when she realized that his shirt was buttoned incorrectly, and one side draped over the zipper of his pants while the other barely covered the dark trail of hair that disappeared behind it. He was smiling and looked adorably mussed, and she crossed her arms. "Well, that's part of it, I guess. But I think we need to really talk about what's going on here with us."

Jamie sobered and nodded. "I'll be honest. I thought we were just going to get busy. But you're right. We do need to talk."

Maya nodded, suddenly feeling awkward. "So, what are we doing here?"

Jamie sat on her bed and ran his hand through his hair. "Maya," he exhaled as she sat next to him. He seemed to search for the right words to use. Maya held her breath. What was he trying to tell her?

"Maya," he started again. "Since that night in the club, when you kissed me, before we'd even actually met really, I wanted you. When I saw you in Dr. C.'s class, I wanted you again. But I'll reiterate, I didn't hire you so I could sleep with you. But since then, I have had to use all of my restraint to not touch you." He turned to her, reaching out to caress her cheek.

"And then Vegas happened. I thought that making love to you was something that needed to happen. As if I could somehow purge my desire for you from my system. But it just made it worse. And since then, I've wanted you every second of every day."

"Jamie." She sighed. "I want you, too."

He pulled her to him and kissed her. "Maya, do you think we could make this work?"

"Make this work?"

"Us," he said. "You and me. Now that I've had you, I can't go back to us just being business associates."

Maya's mind raced. "Jamie, you want a relationship with me?"

His hands grasped her face, and he pulled her away slightly so he could look into her eyes. "Yes. I want to be with you, Maya. Is that what you want?"

"It is," she admitted. "But there's something I'm worried about."

He looked at her with the obvious questions in his eyes.

She hesitated and took a deep breath. "If we're in a relationship, and people know it, there's no way that anyone would take me seriously. They would think I was just some little tart that you hired to help you relieve a little tension during your workday. And if I'm promoted or get another job, people will think that I just got it because

of you and some connections, some strings you pulled."
Maya moved away from his grasp to sit up straight. "And
my career, my future, is too important to me to mess up."

Jamie sat back and looked at her. He nodded and
frowned. "Maya, I would never want to do anything
that would hurt you, personally or professionally. But
this—" he gestured between the both of them "—is too
important, too big for us to ignore. I've never craved another woman like I do you. We can be so good together."

"God, Jamie, I want this, too," she whispered.

"Why don't we give us a chance, but we'll keep it
private. It'll be just for us. That way, nobody will judge
or come down hard on either of us. It won't affect your
career, and God knows I can't afford any negative pub-
licity right now."

Maya nodded. "Okay. But do you think we can keep
it secret?"

"We can do anything." Jamie leaned into her. He
kissed her softly and it took her breath away.

They were still sitting on her bed, and Jamie's fingers were at the buttons of her blouse. He undid each one
leisurely, torturously slow, until he reached the bottom
and swept the shirt from her shoulders, and it fell to her
mattress. Her room was cool and small bumps rose on
her arms. Jamie must have noticed, because as his lips
found hers once again, he put his hands on her shoulders
and brought his palms down her arms until he reached
her hands and held them tightly. It was such a sweet, romantic gesture that she could have cried, but his clever
mouth was too busy distracting her.

Jamie lowered his attention to her neck and shoulders.
His lips tracked delicate kisses across the hollows of her
collarbone as she sighed. He had a delicious, magical

mouth. His hands wandered freely, lightly brushing her bra straps aside. She reached back and unclasped it, allowing him access to her breasts. He took them into his hands and waiting mouth hungrily. He feasted on her sensitive nipples, taking each tip alternately between his lips. She moaned and arched her back so that her chest pushed into his face. She grasped the hair at the back of his head and held him in place, not wanting to be apart from him for even a moment.

He rose slightly, pushing her shoulders to the bed so that he lay on top of her. She bit her bottom lip in anticipation of what was to come when his lips, tongue and teeth dragged down her midsection, over her tight belly, until he reached the waist of her skirt. He flicked open the button, and she obediently raised her hips to help him slide the material down her thighs.

Maya lay on her bed, clad in only her filmy, lace panties. He looked over her appreciatively and then resumed his oral ministrations, as he hooked the lace at her hips with his fingers and slowly lowered them as well, until she was fully exposed to him. She bit back a moan as his lips met the apex of her thighs. She threw back her head, eyes closed, and let her body be completely overtaken by this man.

"Jamie," she gasped when his mouth opened over her and his tongue and fingers spread her folds and delved inside. His touch was magic. Under his masterful skill, she felt as though she was floating above the bed, as if she'd come out of her body. With each breath against her skin, each swipe of his tongue, she felt herself go higher and higher. She pictured herself looking down at the image that they must have presented. Her naked on her bed with Jamie's dark head between her legs, driving her insane.

She felt her orgasm build, one hand gripping his hair and the other twisting the bedsheet in her fist. She simultaneously attempted to get closer to his mouth and to desperately break free of the delicious torture. Her eyes were closed and she heard, and felt, Jamie's growl echo throughout her body, as he roughly clasped his hands on her hips to keep her with him. His strength was all she needed, as she cried out and shook with the tremors of her orgasm. Jamie stayed with her until the quakes subsided and he slowly slipped up her body, showering her still quaking body with light kisses until he reached her lips. She kissed fiercely. His taste mingled with her own, making for a heady experience. Exhaustion overtook her and her eyes fluttered shut, despite her attempts to keep them open. She reached for the front of his slacks to the hard length of him and she stroked him. She could barely keep her eyes open but she wanted to return the favor. He chuckled and removed her hands and he pulled the blankets over her.

"Not tonight," he whispered, standing. She grew cold in his absence and pulled her blanket to her chin.

"But—"

"Don't argue, you can get me next time," he laughed.

"Where are you going?" she asked, her eyes closed.

"I'm not going anywhere, just getting undressed." She heard the rustle of his clothing hitting the floor as he joined her in bed. "I'm staying right here."

19

JAMIE HEARD THE incessant buzz of Maya's cell phone alarm clock. He rolled over and buried his face in her hair. "Time?"

"Six." She yawned, turning and curling into his side.

He felt her warmth and pulled her closer. They had only been asleep for a few hours, yet he'd slept better than he had in a long time. They slept close, which was the only way her smallish bed would allow them.

Jamie groaned. "Why don't you call in sick?"

"Oh, I would." She turned in his arms to face him, not caring about him seeing her bed head or smelling her morning breath. "But my boss is a tyrant. Do you know he had me working till about one o'clock this morning?"

Jamie chuckled into her hair. "That guy sounds like a real despot."

"Yeah, but he makes up for it by having a really sexy body, and a devious mouth."

He pulled her hips closer to him. She could feel the length of his hard erection against her hip. He groaned and took another look at the clock. "We don't have time to do this, do we?"

"No, but we'll probably do it anyway." She laughed.

"You're quite right. But, hey, I'm the boss. I can come in a little later if I want," he said, rolling her under him and kissing her again. "You're the one who will have to kiss ass to make up for being late."

JAMIE WALKED INTO his office about ninety minutes later than normal. It didn't escape Mary's careful eye.

"You're late."

"I'm the boss, Mary. I'm allowed," he said curtly. "Especially after the hours I've been putting in. I guess I needed a little extra sleep this morning."

"Yes, of course you did. Although, Maya was also late this morning. I guess she needed a little sleep, as well," she finished with a side-eye glance.

"Well, she's been here with me every night, working the same hours as me. I think we can give her a little leeway on that minor infraction, don't you think?"

"We sure can, Jamie. Here are your messages." She handed off a small stack of paper. "And you've got that meeting with the board in an hour."

"Thanks," he said, pushing through the door to his office. He saw Maya sitting at her desk. He smiled, recalling the emptiness he'd felt leaving her bed. He practically had to force himself out of her room in order to head to his own apartment to shower and change before work. He had wanted to stay. He had wanted to wrap himself up in her, cocooned in her tiny bed, in her tiny room. But she insisted he leave so they would actually get to work.

Maya looked up and met him with a bright smile of her own. He strode over to her and without a word he pulled her into a kiss. He once again felt himself harden. How could he want her again? It was then that he realized that if he could somehow manage to be away from her, he should arrange for her to have her own office. How would he get anything done otherwise?

As if she could read his thoughts, Maya pulled away. "Come on, we're already late getting started. We've got too much to do today."

"Fine," he said, wrenching himself away from her with a grimace. "Let's get to work."

20

JAMIE WAS PLEASED with the way work had been progressing on the hotels in both Montreal and Las Vegas, and he and Maya had become a powerful team in both the boardroom and in bed. They had managed to keep their relationship a secret, and if anyone suspected that something was up, thankfully, it was never voiced. But as far as he could tell no one was the wiser.

While the Las Vegas property was still in progress, the Montreal hotel was nearing completion, and it was time for Jamie to begin forming a management team to run it, and he hadn't any doubts about who should be in charge of it. He knew that Maya would be perfect in the role, but he hadn't had a chance to discuss it with her yet, but he figured that he would wait until they got closer to the opening date, before the press conference they would use to announce the grand opening.

He and Maya were having lunch when he decided to tell her. He looked across the table at her. They kept a professional distance, while under the tablecloth he felt Maya's foot begin a slow glide up his leg. That was one of the things he enjoyed about her, her sexy impulsive-ness. It wasn't a side of herself that she promoted or exhibited in public, but in private she was a dynamo. When she wasn't 100 percent focused on work, that is. She was saucy with a highly erotic side.

"Maya," he started. "I've got something I want to propose."

"Oh?" she asked with a small, but wicked, smile. "What's on your mind?"

He reluctantly removed her foot from his groin. "Maya, this is serious."

Her smile disappeared, and she sat up straight in her chair. "Okay, what's up?"

"Maya, you know we're looking into staffing the local hotel now. The manager needs to know the ins and the outs of the industry, J. Sellers Holdings and how we do business."

"Makes sense."

"And, Maya, I can't think of anyone more capable of running the hotel than you."

Maya paused, speechless for several beats. "Jamie, I don't know. I've got no experience in that type of role."

"Hear me out," he pleaded. "You have the education, the skills, the connections, the intuition and the fortitude to do this. If there's anything you need, I'll be right there with you. This is a great opportunity for you."

Maya was silent as she looked everywhere in the restaurant but at him. Jamie felt the tension rise. "Say yes."

"Jamie." Maya's voice lowered to a dangerous whisper, and she leaned across the table. "This is exactly what I was afraid would happen. You're offering me this position, to run your flagship hotel—"

"That's right," Jamie said, unwavering.

"This is a job I want someday, but it isn't one I'm qualified for right now. What would people say? How am I supposed to know if it's because I'm actually qualified, or because I'm sleeping with you?"

Jamie saw red. Did she really think that he would risk his business reputation and his integrity to put a person in charge just because he was seeing her? He also leaned forward, but kept his voice even and low. It still appeared as if they were having a pleasant business lunch. "How dare you, Maya. How dare you question my integrity like that. You should know that I do not conduct business with my cock. That's a dangerous and irresponsible way to run a company. I want you to run the hotel because I know you're right for the job, not because I've been inside of you. Are we clear?" he asked her after a beat.

Maya was speechless for a moment. "Jamie, I'm sorry. I panicked." She picked up her fork and fiddled with the tablecloth a little. He could almost see the gears turning in her head. Obviously, she was debating the repercussions of what he had asked her. "Do you really think I can do the job?"

He reached across the table in a risky display of affection to put his hand over hers. "I wouldn't have offered it to you if I didn't."

With a large exhale, she nodded. "All right," she said quietly. "All right, I'll do it."

THE ENERGY HAD changed between them when they returned to the office. Maya was more distant. More serious. Would she halt their relationship in light of her promotion? Jamie hoped to hell not. He wouldn't be able to be near her if he couldn't have her. When he closed the office door behind them, however, his fears were allayed.

He felt her hand on his behind, giving a firm squeeze. "Hey," he chuckled, about to turn to her.

"Stop talking," she commanded, putting her hands on his shoulders as she pushed Jamie down in his desk chair and straddled his lap. His hands ran down her back and cupped her behind. She extricated herself and stood. Her eyes transmitted fire into his. He had never seen such exquisite beauty before him, and he groaned in appreciation of her.

He watched her smile as her saucy pink tongue swept her bottom lip. He wanted that tongue in his mouth, which watered with the desire to kiss her. His eyes dropped from her mouth to her perfect body as she reached behind her back to slowly lower the zipper on her dress. She pushed the cap sleeves from her shoulders and let the dress fall to pool around her stiletto-clad feet.

She stood before him, wearing nothing but a blue bra, matching lacy panties and black heels. The sunlight from the wall-sized window behind the desk lit her skin. She walked toward him and dropped to her knees between his spread legs. Her fingers made quick work of his belt, and she unfastened his pants.

"Maya, you don't have to do this," he rasped.

"I'm doing this because I want to. Not because you offered me a job." She paused for a beat. "Are we clear?" She looked up at him from under her long eyelashes as she repeated his earlier words.

"As crystal." He nodded.

"And I don't ever want you to think that. Anything we do on this side of our relationship is because we want to, right?" She tugged on his waistband, and he lifted his hips in compliance so she could bring his pants lower. "And not because of business."

When his boxers reached his thighs, his cock sprang free. She licked her lips and pressed a chaste kiss to the head. Not taking his eye off her, he breathed out quickly, and when her lips parted over the crown, taking him into her mouth, he couldn't stop the shudder that captured his entire body.

"God, Maya," he groaned, wrapping a fist in her hair, and was torn between letting her set the pace and taking complete control to force himself deeper.

She hummed as she went lower, taking all of him in her mouth. The vibration racked through his body. As she continued her work in his lap, Jamie realized as he watched her, that he was in trouble. He had never felt this way about a woman before. He was falling in love with her.

21

WITH THE PRESS GATHERED, Jamie took his spot behind the podium on the DJ stage at Swerve Nightclub in front of the reporters to announce the opening of the hotel.

"Ladies and gentlemen, welcome to Swerve. I was born, raised and educated here in Montreal. This historic city is where I opened my first nightclub, the original Swerve Nightclub, where we stand today. I've since expanded my business and opened successful clubs all over the country." Jamie smiled broadly as he savored the moment. He was about to make one of the most important announcements of his career.

"But I am very proud to tell you that we are all about pushing the envelope and taking it one step further." He gestured to Maya as she started the slide-show presentation behind him. "I am pleased to officially announce the opening of the first of what I hope to be many Swerve Hotels, located right here in Montreal!"

The audience applauded appreciatively as Jamie explained the concept of the hotel and the amenities. He brought Maya forward. "I would also like to introduce the woman who will be running the show here at the downtown hotel—Maya Connor."

Maya waved and approached the podium. She'd prepared a speech. But as she opened her mouth, a voice from the crowd interrupted her.

"Maya Connor," a loud male called out. Because of the spotlights in her eyes, she couldn't find the source. "Can we assume that this new position is directly related to a position you found yourself in just yesterday?"

Maya and Jamie exchanged a confused look. "I'm sorry? What are you talking about?" The lights dimmed and she watched as security agents made their way to the center of the crowd.

The source of the interruption, she now recognized as John Power, was gradually pulled out of the crowd by security. The man responsible for the nastiest, most disparaging stories about Jamie, yelled as he was dragged away by the bouncers. "I'm talking about the video that was uploaded to *Montreal Secrets* yesterday, showing you on your knees, servicing Mr. Sellers. I guess that's how you got the job, huh? Through a job of your own?" he finished with a smirk, obviously proud of his own wit.

JAMIE GROWLED AND stalked off the stage, running so that he would come face-to-face with their accuser. Jamie looked him square in the eye and addressed his security. "Let him go," he ordered them.

"Boss, we're about to throw him out on his ass."

"Let him go, I'm not going to break the jaw of a guy who is being restrained. How would that look?" He pulled back his fist, but before he could inflict any damage, he felt a soft, but firm grasp on his arm.

"Jamie, no," Maya cried. "He isn't worth it."

When Jamie saw Maya's pleading eyes, he dropped his fist.

"Yeah, Jamie, I'm not worth it." John mimicked Maya.

Jamie exhaled and looked at his bouncers. "Just get him the hell out of here." And the two large men dragged the reporter through the stunned, whispering crowd.

AFTER THE DISASTER that was the press conference, Jamie and Maya sat at opposite ends of Trevor's office in the nightclub. The office was their easiest escape route from the madness of the night and the catastrophic press conference. Jamie's hand covered his mouth and the lower half of his face. He kept stealing glances at Maya, who stared at her balled up fingers in her lap.

Trevor was at his laptop. "Here it is, guys, do you want to see it?"

"Yes," Jamie said firmly, while Maya still said nothing.

Jamie had no idea what she was thinking. She wouldn't look at him, so he knew that it couldn't have been good. He sat in front of the computer as Trevor pushed Play.

"Hello, Montreal," the administrator of the *Montreal Secrets* site screeched from the computer speakers. The administrator of the site was a close partner to John Power and they often worked together in collecting and reporting "news."

"Boy, do we have an exclusive for you today," he continued. "This is a brand-spanking-new video of Jamie Sellers which arrived in my in-box from an *anonymous source* this morning." The administrator was in his element. "And I have to tell you all that it is *extremely* not safe for work." Jamie watched as the video switched from the admin's face to a clip in which Maya was visibly on her knees in front of him. A pixelated square covered his cock and a portion of her face. His head was thrown back and his eyes were closed and his hand rested on the back of her head. It was painfully obvious what they were doing in the video that seemed to be taken through the large window behind his desk, with some sort of telescopic lens.

The voice on the video continued. "The woman has since been identified as Maya Connor, Jamie's assistant—"

At the mention of her name, Maya let out a small noise, part exclamation and part sob, from the corner of the room. It got Jamie's attention and he could tell that she was crying. Ignoring the computer screen, he went to her, while Trevor discreetly let himself out of the room.

"—announced today that she would be running Sellers's new Montreal hotel. I'll bet we all know how she got that job."

He stood by her and put his hand on her shoulder. But upon hearing that last remark, he refused to listen to any more. He went back to the desk and picked up Trevor's laptop and hurled it across the room. He saw Maya flinch against the noise and the violence of his actions, and regretted letting his emotions take over.

He went back to her and fell to his knees in front of her. He put his hands on her face, cupping her cheeks. "Maya, I'm so sorry." She remained silent. "Say something to me, please."

"How did this happen?" she asked him quietly, her large eyes filled with tears.

How did it happen? How could I let it happen? He felt responsible. He should have stopped her. He should have known that there was a chance they could have been seen through the large window in the office. "Baby, I don't know what happened. I guess someone saw us in the window, took a video." He brushed a tear from her cheek. "But we'll find him. I swear. I'm going to find who did this to us."

She looked at the floor and not at him, and she whispered, "Jamie. I—I can't work for you anymore."

Even if she'd hit him with a semi, she couldn't have dealt a harder blow. "What do you mean?"

"Jamie, this is exactly what I was afraid would happen. Our *supersecret* relationship was outed, in the worst possible way. For God's sake, it looks like I traded sex for a promotion." She shook her head, and the tears flowed once again. "Jamie, I quit."

Jamie took her face in his hands. "I won't let that happen, Maya. I'll tell them. I'll tell them that we're together, and that you are the best candidate for the job. Who cares what people think?"

"I care, Jamie!" she emphatically stated. "I care. This is my reputation, my career we're talking about. I told you how important my name is to me. It's all I have, and now it's ruined."

"It's not. Maya, we can still make this work," he pleaded.

"No, Jamie. You have to let me go."

Jamie knew that she wasn't just talking about the job. She was leaving him. He pulled his hands from her face and stood. He walked away from her and faced the wall. She was the woman he loved, but his stupid, male pride wouldn't beg her to stay. If she wanted to go, she could go.

Maya sat silent for a moment, and he could feel her eyes on his back. He wouldn't turn to face her. Lest he shed the tears that burned his eyes and threatened to fall onto his cheeks. He wouldn't turn around when he heard her sniff quietly, pick up her purse and walk out the door and out of his life.

22

MAYA LEFT TREVOR'S OFFICE, passing him on the way out. It looked like he was texting someone. She noticed him trying to catch her eye and she ignored him, lowering her head and continuing out the hallway. She went upstairs to Jamie's office to pack her belongings, ignoring the stares and curious glances of her former coworkers.

When she arrived at her apartment, Maya was hoping that Abby wouldn't be home. She really could have used a little more time to curl up in a ball and cry on her bed before she forced herself to pull it together and get her life back in order. No such luck. When she opened the door to the apartment, Abby ran to meet her.

"Maya, honey. I'm so sorry this happened to you." She wrapped her arms around Maya's shoulders and relieved her of the box that held the items from her desk. "What's all this?"

"I packed up my desk. I just had to get out of there."

"What do you mean? What happened?"

"I quit. I couldn't stay. Everyone thinks…" She couldn't bring herself to finish the thought. "Everybody knows…" She looked at her friend. "How did you find out?"

"Trevor told me," Abby answered simply.

Maya thought it was odd that Abby and Trevor were in contact, but she was too exhausted, and too wrapped up in her own drama to question it.

"Maya, everybody knows that you are a wonderful, intelligent woman and that's why Jamie promoted you. Not because of any relationship you have, which, by the way, is also no secret to anyone." Abby led Maya to the couch and passed her a glass that held a small amount of amber liquid.

"Maya, you know how these things go. This will all blow over. You have to believe it. If anyone knows about this kind of thing, it's Jamie. The press has put him through the wringer before, but he always comes back stronger. He can help you with this. Be a united front for the company," Abby pleaded with her. "You can't give this up. This is your dream."

Maya shook her head, determined not to cry. "Abby, I can't. I'm not like him. I'm not well-known, rich or respected. Especially as a woman in this field. All I have is my name. This type of scandal could follow me for the rest of my career. I had to quit, and hopefully I can repair some of the damage that's been done."

Abby nodded and pulled Maya close to herself. "Does Jamie know you left?"

Maya nodded and sniffed. "He does."

"And he didn't try to stop you?"

Maya recalled their conversation in Trevor's office. He'd held her, looked into her eyes and told her that they could make it work. It'd be okay. They could face it together. But when she walked out of the office, away from him, he hadn't stopped her from leaving.

She shook her head, tears fresh from mourning the

loss of her relationship with him. "He wanted to stop me, I know it. But he didn't."

"So, why did you leave him, then?"

Maya didn't know for sure. "It felt like it was my only choice."

"Instead of talking about it? Instead of sticking it out together?"

Maya flinched under Abby's inquisition. "Why are you attacking me?" she asked her friend angrily.

Abby put a firm, but supportive hand on her shoulder. "Honey, I'm always on your side. But this is something you do. When the going gets tough, you get out. It's like when you have something worth fighting for, you don't even see it. That's your MO. I've seen you do this a thousand times. If this was a tough assignment, you would double down and push through it, but when something gets too real, or too emotional, you call it quits. You do so well in an academic or professional setting, but your personal life is a mess."

"That isn't what's going on here."

"No? All right, Maya. If you say so."

THANKFULLY, TREVOR GAVE him a few minutes alone before he made his way back into the office.

"So that went…" Trevor noticed the broken heap on the floor that was once his computer. "Well."

Jamie dismissed it. "I'll buy you a new one."

"Yeah, a better one, too. Thankfully, I've got everything backed up. So, ah…" He sat at his desk, leaned back and laced his fingers behind his head. "What's going on here?"

Jamie remained silent.

"So, you and Maya, huh? I can't say that I'm surprised. I kind of figured there was something going on there with the two of you…"

"What do you know about it?" Jamie grumbled, running an impatient hand through his hair. He'd messed up. He should have been more careful. He had known that they were in front of the window. He shouldn't have let this happen.

"Dude, talk to me. I'm your friend. Where did she go?"

"She left. I don't know where she is."

"You didn't go after her?"

"Nope. She wanted to leave."

"And you let her?"

Jamie smashed his fist down on Trevor's desk. "What was I supposed to do?"

"You obviously care about her. You should have convinced her to stay."

"Dammit, Trevor. I tried!"

"I don't believe you. You're Jamie-goddamn-Sellers." Trevor's adoption of Maya's new nickname for his friend drove the point home. "You have never let anything stand in the way of anything you've ever wanted. You wanted to open a nightclub? You did. You wanted to open twelve? You did. You wanted hotels? You got 'em. She went out on a limb to be with you, and she got burned," he said, getting in Jamie's face. "Fight for her."

Jamie brought his fingertips to his eyes and rubbed them. "She's gone," he sighed. "It's too late."

23

AFTER SEVEN DAYS of crying over Jamie, Maya decided it was time to pick up her life and start fresh. She stayed in her apartment, as the one time she'd left, she was hounded by gossip and tabloid "reporters," who were questioning her relationship with Jamie, what she did to *earn* her promotion and her hasty departure from the company.

She hadn't spoken to Jamie. If she did, she was afraid that she would fall back under his spell. She would go back to work for him, and always live under the shadow of the scandal.

Maya needed a fresh start.

Abby walked into the living room and saw Maya sitting on the couch. "How are you?"

"I'm okay."

"Yeah, it looks like you showered and everything today," Abby joked.

"I'm starting over. Starting today," Maya stated with a smile.

"That's awesome. Glad to hear you're pulling out of your funk."

"Yeah," Maya agreed, a thoughtful smile on her lips. "I think I need a montage."

"A montage?"

"Yeah, you know, like in those cheesy eighties movies. I need clips of me getting my life back in order—me hanging out with friends, me searching online job ads, me going to the gym, picking up kickboxing, going on job interviews. I just wish I could fast-forward through putting myself back together and just be *me* again."

Abby laughed. "You're a nut. You must be feeling better," she said, pulling lightly on Maya's ponytail, and left the room.

Yes, she was feeling better. Maya had a new plan. She needed to go somewhere the scandal wouldn't follow her. She picked up her laptop and started scouring online job ads. She thought about relocating to the other end of the country when one ad in particular caught her eye. The general manager of Blue Hotel and Casino in Las Vegas was looking for an assistant manager. She opened another internet window and quickly searched for any information for Blue, only to discover it was a property that was owned by Garrett Collins.

In a moment of inspiration, she picked up her phone and scrolled through her contacts until she found the one she needed. She dialed and waited for the male voice to answer.

"Garrett Collins's office, Andre speaking."

"Andre? Hey, it's Maya Connor calling, from Montreal. I'm—I was Jamie Sellers's assistant. We met in Vegas."

"Oh, Maya, yes, of course. How are you?"

"I'm great," she lied. "I'm actually calling you because I'm looking to relocate and I just saw the job ad for the assistant manager for Blue."

"Thinking about heading to the desert? Why don't you just email your résumé to me and I'll see that HR gets it, along with a recommendation from the Big Man. You made quite an impression on Garrett when you were here."

Maya found herself smiling. She'd made an impression on Garrett Collins? "Thanks, Andre, I'll be sure to do that."

As Maya said her goodbye and hung up the phone she smiled. She still felt a flicker of apprehension, however. What if Garrett or someone in his human resources department ran a Google search on her? What if they found the video? Her smile faded. There was nothing she could do. The video was out there; she had resigned herself to that fact. And if Garrett Collins saw it, she would have to deal with the situation when it came up. He would hire her or not. But Maya needed a new start. This was just the sort of change she needed to turn her life around.

JAMIE SAT IN his office, once again unable to take his eyes off the empty desk in the corner of the room. Maya was gone, and he missed her desperately. He found it difficult to focus on any of the work that needed his attention. Jamie never thought it would be possible for a woman to make him feel so hollow. When the phone rang, he snapped out of his daydreams and picked it up.

Mary's cool voice came over the intercom. "Jamie, it's Garrett Collins."

"Collins? Really?" Garrett Collins was the last man that Jamie had expected to hear from. Sure, they'd had a pleasant enough introduction and meeting in Las Vegas, but Jamie couldn't imagine what Collins wanted that warranted a one-on-one phone call. "Put him through."

Jamie cleared his throat. "Jamie Sellers here."

"Jamie," said the confident baritone of one of the most successful men in America. "It's nice to speak with you again."

"Well, I can assure you the pleasure is all mine," Jamie replied, still more than a little confused. "What can I do for you today?"

"Well, Jamie, I'm looking for a recommendation from you."

"Okay." Jamie dragged out the word, still not really sure what Garrett was getting at.

"For your assistant, Maya. I received a copy of her résumé today in response to an ad my office placed."

"Really?" Jamie was angry, but he forced himself to control his emotions.

"Yes, I take it she's no longer working for you? Andre tells me that she's looking for a change in scenery. Really, I don't know why she would trade the history and culture of your fine city for the desert, but that's beside the point."

So Maya had reached out to Collins and had contacted Andre. Andre had flirted with Maya incessantly during their trip to Las Vegas. Jamie clenched a fist and imagined that weasel Andre being in the same room as his Maya. His Maya. He shook his head. *She's not yours any longer.* And she no longer worked for him, so she could go anywhere or speak to anyone she pleased.

It also seemed that Garrett Collins had not yet got wind of the scandal that had rocked them and imploded their relationship, which was good news for Maya. But Jamie saw himself as having two choices in the matter.

If he was an evil man, he could absolutely screw Maya. He could sabotage her chance of getting the position, or any others, thereby forcing her to return to work for him. But he wasn't that kind of person. He would obviously tell the truth, praise her to a potential employer, especially one that could further her career, get her out of Montreal and make all of her dreams come true. Jamie did the right thing, even though it meant that he would be permanently removing Maya from his life.

"That's correct. Maya and I have parted ways. Amicably, of course. She was an amazing assistant, intelligent and very capable. She's just looking for something different right now. And if you hire her, you definitely will not regret it."

"That's some glowing praise there, Sellers. Makes me wonder why you didn't keep her for yourself."

Jamie closed his eyes, the stabbing pain in his chest too much to bear. "I would have if she let me, Garrett," he said softly. "Good luck with your interviews. I've got to go now."

24

Maya was washing dishes, elbow-deep in warm, tepid, greasy water. *Ah, the glamorous life.* She had found some high energy dance music to try to drown out her feelings about Jamie, about leaving Montreal, about the job in Vegas she hoped she would get.

There was a loud bang on the door, and she hesitated before removing her rubber gloves and walking to the door. The person on the other side rapped loudly once again. "I'm coming," she hollered out. She hated impatient people. When she got to the door, she looked into the peephole. Jamie stood on the other side. His hands fisted on his hips and a deep scowl on his face. She opened the door and he stormed in.

"Vegas?" he yelled. "You're moving to Vegas?"

"Maybe. I don't know. I applied for a job there with Garrett Collins, but I haven't had an interview scheduled or anything," she stammered. "How did you know?"

"Garrett called me for my recommendation. I can't believe you didn't tell me you were considering moving to Las Vegas. But I guess that would have involved speaking to me at all. You won't return my calls or even have the courtesy to send me a text message."

"What did you say to Garrett?"

"I told him that he would be lucky to have you working for him. And that was it. He didn't mention the video. He didn't even really care why I was letting you go."

"Really?"

"Yes, of course."

"Thank you."

Jamie shook his head and spoke softly. "It's just the truth, Maya."

Maya sighed. Shame creeped over her features. She'd hurt him. She hadn't even thought about his feelings, but it just occurred to her that she wasn't the only one who was in pain. "Jamie, I'm really sorry for how all of this went down."

Jamie shook his head. "Me, too." He exhaled. "I better go."

Maya held back the tears that burned her eyes. "Okay."

"Good luck with the job."

"Thanks," she told his back as he flung open the door and strode quickly into the hallway, and out of her life.

25

MAYA TOOK HER seat on the airplane. Economy this time. This trip to Las Vegas wasn't on the dime of J. Sellers Holdings. That was the difference. Well, that and the fact that she had only purchased a one-way ticket.

Garrett Collins had called her personally to extend the job offer. He'd told her that Jamie's recommendation had been enough for him to hire her, without even having an interview. She'd accepted without question, and her career was once again her primary focus. Working as Jamie's assistant had been an amazing opportunity. She'd had the opportunity to work on some big projects and meet some very important people, Garrett Collins, included. But with an MBA, it was a position below her education. She was more suited to the resort assistant manager position she would be walking into.

Maya sighed unhappily, still missing Jamie—his voice, his scent, his humor, those intense blue eyes, his perpetual five o'clock shadow—and she wondered if the hollow feeling in her chest would ever go away. Maya shook her head, hoping to clear the thoughts from her head; otherwise it would be a long five-hour flight.

Looking at her seat neighbor, the old woman kindly smiled back. She recalled the last time she had flown to Vegas. How Jamie had held her hand and helped her control her fear of flying. Her heart ached at the memory.

As the plane began its taxi down the runway, she closed her eyes. She was about to leave everything behind—the city she'd called home, her comfortable apartment, Abby. Jamie. She was leaving Jamie behind. Focusing on everything she would be gaining from the move helped her feel a little better. Also, she welcomed the Las Vegas heat. No more Montreal winters, no more cold weather.

No more Jamie. Stop it, Maya!

Maya squared her shoulders and shored up her resolve. I can do this. She could get through this flight. She could get through her life without Jamie in it. Breathing deeply, she hoped that the Dramamine she had taken would kick in soon. The sooner she could be in Vegas, and away from Montreal, the better. She was ready to start her new life.

"JAMIE, YOU HAVE got to stop moping over Maya."

Jamie looked up from his tablet and at Trevor, who stood on the other side of the bar holding a clipboard and completing his daily inventory count before the bar opened for business. Jamie was sitting at the bar, nursing a drink and discussing design plans for Swerve Las Vegas via email with Gwen Seaver, the designer he'd hired to oversee the hotel project in Vegas.

"I'm not moping," he corrected his friend, looking back down at his screen. "I'm working."

"Any reason why you're doing it at my bar instead of in your own office?"

"Aren't you the one who says I spend too much time in my office?" he countered. "I'm just interested in a change of scenery in my own bar. Is that okay?" Jamie wouldn't share with his friend that his own office, while quite large, felt confining as of late. It was a room where he greatly felt Maya's presence, so the bar had become a haven of sorts for him.

"Fine by me. But make sure you're gone before opening. Nobody's going to have any fun if you're scowling at anyone who comes near you."

Jamie furrowed his brow. "I'm not scowling. It's just that all of this design stuff is getting to me. It's something I would have had Maya overseeing."

"So no luck hiring her replacement?"

Jamie frowned. *How could I ever replace her?* He must have interviewed two dozen candidates. But not one had come close to filling the void that Maya had left in his life. Professionally speaking, of course. Maya was a fantastic assistant, and it would be hard to find somebody as good as her to work for him. Romantically, however, he didn't think he would ever be able to find another to take her place. He was certain he knew that he would never again attempt to pursue a romantic relationship with anyone under his employ.

"I've had no luck yet."

"Do you think your standards might be a little high?"

"I've never compromised my professional standards. I hire only the best, as you can attest. I simply haven't found the right person yet," he insisted. "And until I do I have to handle all of these details myself." Jamie placed his tablet on the bar and ran his hands through his hair.

Trevor glanced down at the still-lit screen and he raised an eyebrow at what he saw. "Dude, you know I don't like to get involved in your other business affairs, but who is that?"

Jamie glanced down and saw the picture that Gwen used for her email profile. "That is Gwen Seaver. She's the designer I hired for the Vegas hotel. She came highly recommended by Garrett."

"I'll bet she did." Trevor whistled as he took in Gwen's strong features and long, red hair. "The woman is a knockout."

"She is," Jamie admitted, halfheartedly.

"Have you met her?"

"Not in person yet, although we do have a scheduled meeting next week when I head out there."

"You're going to Vegas next week?" Trevor asked.

"Yeah."

"Are you going to see Maya?"

"I hadn't planned on it." Jamie was still too raw. The hurt still too new. There was no way he could possibly even think about seeing her during his trip.

"Probably for the best," Trevor agreed. "But oh man—" he pointed to the picture of Gwen on his screen "—you should get on that, though. A woman like that could make a man forget all sorts of things. And get over the woman who broke his heart."

Jamie frowned at his friend. But he admitted to himself that Trevor might be right. Sure, Gwen had exhibited more than just a professional interest in working with him. The woman had all but propositioned him, asking if he wanted to get together, outside of work, during his next visit, *for drinks and anything else that might happen*, she'd said. He was reluctant to begin a physical relationship with her, but she had guaranteed her discretion.

Maybe a quick fling was just what he needed. A way

to get Maya off his mind. It's not like Gwen was his employee, exactly, and Vegas was certainly far enough away from Montreal, where the scandal had rocked his life. He nodded. "You might be right."

Picking up his glass, he downed the rest of his drink and picked up his tablet. He looked at Gwen's picture. She was a beautiful woman, and he could do a lot worse for a fling. But he couldn't help but feel that it would be like a betrayal to Maya. He shook his head. No. Maya was no longer in his life, and they hadn't spoken in weeks. *She's even living in another country, for God's sake.* Maybe a fling was exactly what he needed to get Maya out of his system. Although, sleeping with Maya in the first place was how he'd planned to get her out of his system. *And you can see how well that worked out for you, Sellers.*

He didn't feel quite right about it. But he needed to move on, get on with his life. With a shaking finger, he clicked on Gwen's profile and set up a date.

26

LAS VEGAS WAS quite different from Montreal. *Understatement of the century, Maya*, she thought as she stepped out of her apartment and into the blazing heat. She'd found it hard to adjust to all of the changes at first. She missed Abby. Her best friend still called and they Skyped whenever they could, but it wasn't the same.

The pace of Las Vegas was also different from that of Montreal. Sure, Montreal was the more populous city, but Las Vegas had far more hustle and bustle. There were always people everywhere, at all hours, coming and going. Tourists stopping for pictures. People drinking and acting out. Maya was more of a quiet person and she didn't care for the rowdiness that came with working on the Strip.

But the first adjustment Maya had had to make was the heat. *Good God, the heat!* She'd always liked warm weather, but when the hot desert sun blazed on her daily, she often found herself seeking the refuge of her air conditioner. To adapt, Maya had been forced to downsize her wardrobe and adopt a business style that was still appropriate, but more suited to the climate. She wore more short skirts and sleeveless blouses these days.

In her new profession, however, she was a natural. She'd adapted so well to the staff, clientele and the organizational culture in only a matter of days, and she also enjoyed an excellent working relationship with Garrett Collins. He was older than Jamie, more experienced and more connected, but she would be lying if she said she didn't miss working with her former lover.

Maya had been there for more than six weeks when Garrett Collins strolled into her office, not bothering to knock, as usual.

He sat on the chair on the opposite side of the desk and crossed his legs. "Maya, I would like you to join me for lunch today." He said it as a statement, not a question. A man like Garrett Collins was not used to asking people to do things.

"Sure, I've got no plans. Any special occasion?"

Garrett shrugged. "Just a meeting with an old friend of yours. Jamie Sellers is in the city to get an update on the progress of his hotel and we arranged to have lunch. Just a friendly get-together."

"Uh, sir, I don't think—" Maya shook her head. She didn't think it would be possible to see Jamie. She still wasn't ready.

"Twelve o'clock sharp at Piazza," he interrupted her, naming the popular restaurant located in the hotel. He strode out the door without glancing back, a man not used to being denied.

Twelve o'clock. Maya had exactly three hours to panic about her upcoming lunch with Jamie. She told Garrett that she had no other plans, and he wouldn't accept any excuse for her absence. *Suck it up, Maya. You're a big*

*girl. You are more than capable of sitting and having a
pleasant lunch with Jamie...* Wasn't she?

WHEN MAYA WALKED into the upscale pizza restaurant,
she found Garrett and Jamie almost immediately. Obviously, when men as influential as those two were in a
room, the power could be felt by all.

Maya took a deep breath and squared her shoulders
and walked toward the table. She smiled, until she saw
that the three of them would not be dining alone. A
beautiful woman was also seated at the table, danger-
ously close to Jamie. She was holding court, both men
captivated, and they hung on to her every word. Maya
thought she might just run away before anyone saw her.
She watched Jamie smile and turn to the woman. Maya
thought she might die.

Jamie was the first to see her. His eyes widened in
surprise for a quick second before he recovered. He
smiled. Maya smiled.

"Maya!" Garrett stood. "You made it."

"Hi." She sat. "Sorry if I'm a little late. I got held up."

"No problem, Maya. We're all just getting here." He
gestured to their female guest. "Maya, this is Gwen.
She's the interior designer I use quite often, and she's
going to be working with Jamie on his hotel."

Gwen extended her hand to Maya and she accepted
it. But she could see through the phony smile that Gwen
plastered on her face—*the woman is clearly a snake*—
but there was no mistaking the possessive hand she had
placed on Jamie's forearm. "Hello, Jamie," she said
coolly, trying to form the words around the lump in
her throat.

At her tone, Jamie's eyebrows lowered to harsh, dark lines. "Maya, how have you been?"

Maya about shivered from the formality of it all. She smiled too broadly, showing too many teeth. She must have looked ridiculous. "Great!" She suddenly turned manic. "Everything's great! I love it here. And the job's keeping me busy. And the weather's great here. How are the plans coming for your new hotel?" All of the words had been spoken in mere seconds. She wanted to kick herself for acting so foolish.

"Fantastically." He turned to Gwen. "I'm actually in town to discuss the concept and design ideas with Gwen here," he said, taking her hand and removing it from his forearm.

Maya smiled to herself, watching the other woman's cocky smile falter. *What do we have here?*

"So, Jamie, what we have here is a blend of white linens with dark hardwood." Gwen scrolled through the images she'd designed on her tablet. "This presents a mix of the cleanliness and the opulence that comes with white, but it also feels kind of rustic, and that's a huge look right now."

Jamie was blown away by Gwen's eye for flair. His eyes were wide in excitement. "This looks amazing, Gwen. I love it."

He took her tablet from her and scrolled through once again on his own. It was finally happening, and if these sketches and designs were any indication, Swerve Las Vegas was going to be absolutely incredible. "Can you email these images to me?" He handed the tablet back to her.

"Yeah, sure," Gwen said, accepting it and sitting back against the couch.

She stretched her arms along the back and crossed her legs toward Jamie in a well-practiced move of seduction that Jamie recognized. She looked at him intently, her voice smooth like velvet. "I'm glad you like it. Now that all the pesky work is out of the way, what do you suggest we do with the rest of this evening?"

Jamie caught the way she looked at him through her eyelashes. And in his pre-Maya days, he might have succumbed to her advances. He averted his eyes and brought his glass to his lips. Maybe pouring them each a scotch when she'd come in was a mistake. There was no mistaking the intent in her eyes and the sexy, catlike way she moved. But Maya still occupied all of the space in his brain. Why had he suggested that they *get together* during his visit?

Jamie smiled uneasily. Suddenly the idea of a quick, meaningless fling with Gwen became less appealing to him. Sure, she was a sexy woman, and he knew that they would both have one hell of a night together, but since seeing Maya earlier that day he had little interest in any other woman.

Sensing his reluctance, Gwen reached out and put a hand on his thigh. "What do you think?" She let her hand move up, up, farther, venturing around to his inner thigh. Every time Maya had touched him during their short relationship, she lit a fire inside of him. But with Gwen, he felt nothing. Well, almost nothing. He was still a man and Gwen was still a gorgeous woman whose warm, soft, but insistent hand was quickly closing in on his cock. Sure, it had been weeks since he'd had sex. Not since Maya had left. But he knew that he couldn't be with Gwen.

Despite his best attempts to discourage her, Gwen looked down and caught sight of the growing bulge behind his zipper and she smiled seductively. "Well, it looks like you have an idea of what we could do."

Jamie took a deep breath and shook his head. He picked up her hand and removed it from his lap. "Gwen, I don't think so. This can't happen."

She shook her head, confused, and then looked pointedly in his lap. "From where I'm sitting it definitely looks like it can."

"No, it's not going to happen." He took a deep breath. "There's someone else."

"Someone else?" she hissed. "You didn't mention this other person when we agreed to get together."

"I know. It's a long story. But, Gwen, I'm sorry, we can't do this."

"I can't believe this," she said, stunned. Jamie was sure that no other man had ever said no to her. "Are you serious? I've heard about you, Jamie. I heard you were a notorious skirt-chaser, and rumor has it that you like to mix business with pleasure, if you know what I'm saying," she said, her voice too loud with astonishment. "I figured you would be a sure thing."

Sudden anger darkened Jamie's features. *Gwen likes to play dirty.* She was trying to draw him out, get a reaction from him. Lashing out in anger because he rejected her advances. He didn't respond, refusing to play along.

Quickly, Gwen changed her mood on a dime. She composed herself and stood languidly from the couch. "Fine. I'm sorry. I'm just a little disappointed, I guess. You know, I skipped the gym this morning and was hoping to make up the cardio." She laughed shakily as she gathered her things. "But, you know, that's life, I guess. I'll email those pictures to you when I get back to my office."

Jamie closed his eyes, relieved that even though he spurned her advances, Gwen would continue to give him her business. "Thank you, Gwen."

"What, did you think I'd quit because you wouldn't sleep with me?"

Jamie laughed still not convinced that he wasn't in trouble with her. "I—"

She walked up to him and placed a hand on his chest and rubbed it back and forth a little. "I'm still a professional. Our personal issues won't affect business."

"That's a relief," he said, escorting her to the door. Her slick smile caused him some concern, and he hoped that he could trust her word that their professional relationship would not be affected. Jamie had met women like her, and they did not care for being rebuked. "Thank you. I'll be in touch." He opened the door and she left without a word.

27

JAMIE STEWED IN his hotel room. He paced like a caged animal. Gwen had just left and he was restless. He was also still agitated from his run in with Maya. A short time ago, Maya had meant the world to him. He had seen every side of her. Kissed her. Made love to her. Now she acted like a complete stranger to him. Her cold indifference at lunch had so infuriated him that after his meeting with Gwen, he had to take the rest of the day off. He just couldn't concentrate.

Gwen would have been a surefire way to release some tension. And he knew it would have been great, too. Maybe that was part of the reason why he was so agitated. His dick didn't seem to understand why neither his brain nor heart wanted to get naked with Gwen. She had been more than eager and willing to lock herself in a hotel room with him to do anything he wanted. And while he was certainly looking forward to it, seeing Maya today had changed his mind. Seeing her had brought everything back—all the longing, the desire. All other women ceased to exist for him. All the while, she sat there, seemingly indifferent to his very existence, as if they hadn't been intimate only a short time ago.

Jaime wasn't much of a drinker. Recent history had proven that if he had a little too much to drink, he lost control. But, figuring he wouldn't be leaving his room anytime soon, he opened the minibar and pulled out all of the small bottles of scotch, and he poured three of them into a short glass. He brought the crystal tumbler to his lips, but a furious pounding on his door stopped his hand before he took a drink. He walked to the door, and when he opened it with an annoyed tug, he found Maya standing on the other side.

He softened. "Maya."

"Hi, Jamie."

"What can I do for you?" He stepped aside to allow her to enter.

She walked farther into the room, not looking directly at him. "Well, I just wanted to talk to you about lunch. I'm sorry if it was awkward. That wasn't my intention. I was hoping that we could at least pretend that we're still friends, at least in social or business situations."

Jamie felt his control snap, and he raised his voice. *How dare she.* "Maya, we could still be friends. We could still be lovers. But you were so stubborn and prideful that the only option you saw fit was to leave the goddamn country."

She flinched at his tone. "Jamie, I had to—"

"None of this had to happen, Maya. We could have moved on from the video. I have a legal team behind us to punish the people responsible. You could have stayed there with me and worked with me."

"You don't understand what it's like for a woman, especially in this business. I needed to step away from you.

I needed that, for me and for my career, so I wouldn't always be the woman who was caught going down on her boss," she argued. She stopped and her eyes shone with unshed tears. "But you let me walk away entirely, Jamie." Her voice broke. "You didn't fight for me."

The sadness etched on her face completely undid him. "Maya, I was stubborn. I was hurt. And believe it or not, that video was embarrassing for me, too. You were waiting for me to make you stay? I could have. I would have. But I was scared, too," he said, his voice cracking a little. He had never admitted fear to another person in his life. But that was what Maya did to him. She broke through and destroyed every one of the walls and barriers that he had been constructing for decades.

She stopped. Eyes wide, mouth agape. "What were you afraid of?"

Jamie took a deep breath, and he looked everywhere before his eyes settled squarely on hers. "I was afraid that I would put it all on the line, and you would walk away, anyway."

Maya sat on the couch in stunned silence. "I thought that seeing that video was the worst moment of my life. But it wasn't. There were so many other awful moments after that. Leaving you in Trevor's office, when you stormed out of my apartment, getting on the plane with my one-way ticket. They were all awful." By now, the tears were steadily flowing down her face.

Jamie went to her and wrapped his arms around her. Nothing had ever felt more right than when she was in his arms. "Maya. I'm not afraid anymore. I don't want to be without you." The words *I love you* were poised at the tip of his tongue. But he couldn't say them. He was still raw and he still wasn't ready to give her all of him.

"I'm not afraid, either. I've stopped running. But my life is here now. My job with Garrett. I just can't leave and go back to Montreal."

"I wouldn't expect you, too. But we can make it work. I promise. We just have to be willing to. Are you willing to work for us, Maya?" Jamie lifted her chin with his fingertips and gazed into her eyes. "With the new hotel opening here, I'll be back and forth. We can see each other whenever I'm in town. We can talk on the phone, text, there's Skype, email. It won't be easy, but I know we can do it. It's worth it."

"It is worth it," she agreed. "We can try to make it work."

Jamie felt the weight he'd carried for weeks lift from his shoulders. He pulled her closer and kissed her, as if he had been apart from her for years. Gathering her in his arms, he stood and carried her to his bed.

Laying her on the bed, his heart pounding in his chest, Jamie stared at Maya. He couldn't believe she was here. In his bed. He never thought he would make love to her again, touch her body, run his fingers through her hair, hear her moan his name…

"Are you actually going to do anything, or just stand there?" she asked, snapping him out of his trance.

He shook his head and laughed. He dropped onto the bed next to her, bringing his lips to hers. He relished it. He had her back and he was not going to lose her again.

28

When Monday morning rolled around, Maya had a definite skip in her step. Early that morning, Jamie had returned to Montreal, but not before spending two amazing days and nights with her at her apartment. She had been happy in Vegas before she and Jamie had rekindled their relationship. But now, everything felt right. As if everything in her life was starting to fall into place.

Jamie had already texted her from his stopover, and she eagerly awaited his arrival at home, when he would call her. She missed his voice, the way he roughly cleared his throat when he wanted her, his breath on her ear... she shivered and mentally shook it off. There would be plenty of time to talk to Jamie tonight, but at the moment she had a full day of work ahead of her. She started by checking her messages, some of which required immediate attention. So she settled into her desk and put all thoughts of Jamie away until later, when she would have time.

It was after midnight when Jamie opened the door to his apartment. He had been traveling for the entire day, and had somehow endured multiple stopovers, bad weather, delays and everything else that could go wrong in what should have been just a five-hour flight. He was exhausted. He did make himself feel better by imagining the evisceration of his corporate travel team and boiling them in oil.

He dropped the thought and his bag by the door and went to the fridge. Grabbing a bottle of water, he pulled out his phone and dialed Maya's number. He wanted nothing more than to go to bed, but not before he heard her voice.

"Hello?" she answered, after several rings.

"Hey, it's me."

"How was your trip?"

"Long, awful," he responded through a yawn.

"You sound exhausted. It's got to be what, almost 1 a.m. there?"

"Yeah."

"You should go to bed. I'm betting you'll be at the office bright and early in the morning, am I right?"

"You're not wrong." He laughed, taking a swallow of water. "And yeah, I'm heading to bed now. I just wanted to talk to you first."

"That's sweet. But why don't you give me a call tomorrow and we'll have a real conversation?"

"Sounds great."

She sighed. "I miss you, Jamie." A sudden sadness crept into her voice.

"I miss you, too. I'll call you tomorrow, okay?"

"Great. I can't wait. Bye."

Jamie hung up the phone with a sigh and went to his bedroom. He was exhausted, but he figured he might as well unpack his bag before he went to bed. That way, he would be able to get his dry cleaning out in the morning. He threw it on the bed and unzipped the bag. He chuckled to himself when lying on top of his light gray suit were a pair of lacy, red panties that he recognized as Maya's.

29

TONIGHT. JAMIE WAS going to reach Maya tonight if he had to stay awake until sunrise. He'd had such a hectic week, and it was made worse by the fact that he had barely been able to connect with Maya. He knew that trying to maintain a relationship despite being a couple of time zones away would be tricky, but he didn't realize that it would be this hard. Even though it was only the difference of a couple hours, it was tough. He needed to speak to her. He felt as if her voice was the only thing that could soothe his frazzled nerves.

He bypassed the bottles of water in his fridge and reached for a beer. Popping it open, he walked to his living room and sat down in the plush leather recliner that he loved. He checked the time on his cell phone: 10 p.m. He calculated the time in Las Vegas and knew it was early evening there. *Perfect.* He knew she had taken the afternoon off to prepare for Abby's visit the next day, so he was sure he would get her at home. He dialed. After only one ring, her voice, sultry on the line, greeted him.

"Hi, Jamie," she whispered.

He smiled. "Maya, I've got you."

"You certainly do."

He settled into his leather chair and leaned back so the leg rest extended. He was almost fully reclined, a broad smile on his face, a beer in one hand and his life-line, Maya, on the phone in the other. For the first time in more than a week, he was finally relaxed. He sighed to himself. "So what are you doing?"

He heard some water splashing from her end. "I'm actually in the bath."

He chuckled and closed his eyes, imagining her in her bathtub. Remembering her the night they'd taken a bath on their first night together in Las Vegas. Her hair pulled back, her skin warm and soft from the bathwater. He was now inspired and decided to play a game. "Really? Do you have any bubbles in there?"

"I do."

"I hear music. What are you listening to?"

"Norah Jones. Helps me unwind."

"How high is the water?"

She moaned a little. "High enough so that it covers the tops of my nipples."

He groaned, imagining her rosy nipples. He licked his lips. "Why don't you give them a little pinch for me?"

He heard her breath in the phone. "What?"

"Just do it. Trust me. Put the phone on speaker. I want you to feel your breasts for me. Pretend your hands are my hands." She was silent. He thought she wouldn't agree. Call him a pervert and hang up. But then he heard the phone shuffling around, a sign that she was doing as he asked. He grinned.

"Okay, the phone's on speaker," she told him, her voice sounded farther away.

"Okay, now do what I asked you to," he commanded her softly.

He heard her moan, and the exquisite sound rattled through him. He felt himself harden in his slacks. "Squeeze your nipples for me, baby."

Her gasp told him that she had. He knew that her nipples were more sensitive than any he'd ever seen. He smiled. "How does that feel, Maya?"

"Amazing."

"Are you still doing it?"

"Yeah."

"Are you imagining that it's me touching you?"

"Yeah," she breathed.

"You know what I would do if I was there right now?"

"What?"

"I would then let my fingers glide down your ribs, over your stomach until they came to rest at your perfect little pussy." Her gasp urged him on. His own hand unbuckled his belt and he unzipped his pants. "Are you wet?"

She giggled. "Well, I am in the bathtub."

He rolled his eyes and laughed with her. "You know what I mean, smart-ass," he said, full of affection. "I'm trying to be sexy here." His hand found his stiff erection. "May we continue?"

"Okay." She stifled her laughter. "Let's continue."

Jamie took a swig of beer and put the bottle on an end table. He put his own phone on speaker and he closed his eyes. "Imagine me slipping my fingers inside you, sliding them along your clit." She moaned. His own hand roughly gripped his rigid cock. God, he wished it was her hand stroking him.

Maya spoke next, her voice a sultry whisper. "Your

own breathing is starting to get a little heavy. Are you touching yourself?"

So she wanted to start playing the game, as well. "I am."

"What are you thinking about?"

"I'm thinking about you. Your mouth and your hands on me."

Maya moaned, her own pleasure apparent. "Mmm... Jamie, did you know that after the first day I came to work with you, I ran a hot bath and I got myself off in the tub?"

"God, Maya," he moaned, his fist working quickly over his now-glistening shaft. If that wasn't the hottest thing he'd ever heard. "You're so sexy."

"Jamie," she gasped. He knew that she was close, that her sensitive body couldn't take so much stimulation. He felt her pending orgasm as if she were in the room with him, as if he were the one bringing her to climax.

Her crescendo matched his and, as they both played with themselves, their pants and moans fueled each other until they both erupted with furious climaxes. Their combined breathing slowed. For a few moments, they both were silent.

When their breathing regulated, Maya was the first to speak. "So, how was your day?" She giggled.

"It's suddenly going a lot better," he said with a laugh. "It's great to actually speak with you. I can't believe we've been missing each other all week."

"I know. The whole time zone thing is really frustrating."

"Yeah, enough about that, though. How about you? How was your day? Got everything squared away for Abby's visit?"

"Yeah, mostly. I've got some show tickets, some table service reserved at a couple of clubs and some great restaurant reservations."

"Sounds like fun. I'm sure you guys are going to have a great time."

"We will. She loves Vegas. And her visit will fill some of the time until you come back."

"Yeah, I'll be there next Wednesday. I've got a couple of meetings lined up with Gwen, though," he added.

"Gwen?"

"The interior designer I've hired for the Vegas hotel. You met her. At that lunch with Collins."

"Oh, right." She paused. "Well, that's okay. As long as I get you the rest of the time."

"You've already got me," he assured her.

Maya sighed on the other end. "I can't wait to see you. But I know it's getting late there, and I should let you get some sleep."

He sighed regretfully, he didn't want to hang up the phone. He wanted to keep her there all night. Hell, he wanted to go to bed with her, hold her in his arms until daylight. "Alright, I guess you're right. I can't wait to see you."

"Me, too."

"Maybe you can run a bath and I can catch the live show of what just happened."

30

WHEN MAYA HEARD the announcement for the arrival of Abby's flight, she couldn't contain her excitement. It had been so long since she'd seen her best friend, and she had worked hard to make the next five days spectacular. She looked around at all of the other people waiting quietly for their loved ones. Maya, however, was bouncing on the balls of her feet, trying to expend some energy while she waited for Abby.

Sure, she missed Jamie, as she hadn't seen him since the weekend that they reconciled, but she missed Abby in a way she couldn't imagine. In missing Jamie, she missed their intimacy, his loving words, his touches, his body. But with Abby, it was completely different. Abby was her best friend in the whole world. She missed having a girlfriend around to share late-night chats, chick flicks and the occasional bottle (or two) of wine. Sure they talked on the phone and with video chat, but it wasn't the same.

She saw Abby's blond pixie cut before she saw the woman herself. She squealed and jumped up and down, and she ran toward her friend, pushing through the throngs of people waiting for their own loved ones as they disembarked.

When she reached Abby, Maya pulled her into a fierce hug, which held all of her feelings and the way she'd missed her friend. "Oh, my God," she cried as she grasped Abby. "I can't believe you're here."

"Oh, I missed you so much," Abby told her, returning her hug with the same fierceness. "Canada—like, the whole country—is not the same without you, Maya. Thank you for inviting me."

"I'm sorry it took this long." Maya held her at arm's length, studying her friend as if, if she didn't look closely, she might find it wasn't actually her, but some stranger. "How was your flight?"

Abby grimaced. "Ugh, next time you score me free tickets to fly here, it'd better be first class. The smelliest man sat next to me. And he had the aisle seat, so I couldn't even get up to go to the washroom. At least the male flight attendant was cute. He kept bringing me free champagne. So I'll admit, I might have already gotten my Vegas vacay started on an appropriate foot, because I might actually be a little bit tipsy," she giggled.

"Good girl," Maya laughed. "Cute flight attendant, huh?"

"I guess he just fell in love with me in my yoga pants and flip-flops combo," she gestured to her traveling outfit.

Maya raised a skeptical eyebrow at Abby. "Girl, you actually look flawless, as usual." She wasn't lying, Abby had an amazing flair for making the most casual and ragtag of outfits look cute and fashionable. If she didn't love Abby so much, Maya would hate her for it.

"Well, why don't we head back to my place and I'll

let you freshen up, as if you need it, and then we can hit your choice of restaurant for lunch. You hungry?"

"Starving," Abby told her as they linked arms and walked toward the baggage claim. "And I can't wait for you to tell me all about your awesome, glamorous new life."

"So how's the job hunt going?" Maya asked Abby as they were seated at a tropical-themed restaurant. They ordered margaritas and shared a plate of nachos and salsa.

"Well, it sucks," Abby replied, dunking a chip. "Everyone from our class is competing for the same positions, and there's not a lot of hiring going on. I tell you, you're pretty lucky, getting that job with Jamie and then getting one out here. It's dog-eat-dog right now."

Maya frowned, she felt bad Abby wasn't having any luck, but a small wave of relief rolled over her that she had made the right decision by taking the job that she was offered. "I'm sorry, Abby."

"Oh, don't be. I'll find something. In the meantime, though, Trevor, from Swerve, has hired me to be a bartender at the club on weekends. I'm not exactly using my MBA, but hey, the money's really, really good, and he's pretty fun to hang out with."

"I hope he isn't replacing me as your new bestie."

"He could never do that," Abby assured her. "But he is quite nice to look at."

"That's good. Trevor is a great guy. He and Jamie are really close."

"They are and, speaking of Jamie, how are things with you two?"

Maya shrugged. "Things are good. Long distance is really hard, though. The time zone is tricky and it feels like we never talk. But he'll be here next week." She sighed. "But, you know, it's like maybe too much distance. I don't know. Some days are really hard, and I don't always think that it's worth it."

"Don't do that," Abby warned, pointing a finger at Maya. "Haven't we had this conversation before? You do this every time. It's like you push away any shot at happiness that you have. You're sabotaging yourself. Unless you honestly don't want to be with Jamie, you have to work for it." Abby took a sip of her margarita. "Love is scary and hard and it's a lot of work, but isn't it worth it?"

"Love?"

"You love Jamie, don't you?"

"I—I don't know. I— Some days I think so, but others… It's just so hard not seeing him every day. He's in Montreal and I'm here."

"Maya, you're too stubborn for your own good. You need to trust your heart. If you love Jamie, it'll be worth it. All this distance won't always be an issue."

Maya remained silent and sipped her margarita. *Do I love Jamie?* After this conversation with Abby, she was even more confused. *Do I sabotage my own happiness? No. I don't, do I?*

IT WAS LUNCHTIME when Maya saw her.

Maya and Abby had spent the previous night at a swanky club, and Maya hadn't fared much better than she had the previous time she'd gone to a club with Abby—the night they'd gone to Swerve. She awoke with a hangover, and she was late for work, and she barely had enough time to pull her hair into a ponytail and apply only a minimal amount of makeup.

In the hallway on the way to her office, Maya popped a couple of ibuprofen and downed them with her coffee, when she saw a flash of red hair approach her. It took her only a moment to place the woman's striking face. It was Gwen Seaver.

"Hi, Gwen," Maya muttered as she walked by her.

Gwen stopped. Her face twisted into confusion. "I'm sorry, have we met?"

Yes, we've met. Maya's eyes narrowed. *And you remember me.* Maya identified this as a game that manipulative people played, belittling the importance of others. "Yes, we have. I'm Maya, the assistant manager of Blue Hotel. You're also working for my friend Jamie Sellers on his hotel."

"Ah, yes, hello, Maya." Gwen shot out her hand. "Nice to see you again."

"Nice to see you, as well," Maya lied.

"So, you and Jamie are friends," Gwen said, with a raised eyebrow.

"Yup, me and Jamie are friends." Maya didn't see the need to explain her relationship with Jamie to this snotty woman.

"He is a great guy." Gwen pursed her lips. "He and I have been working *very closely* as of late."

Maya cocked her head to the side. "What?"

"Yeah, it's a big project, we've worked quite a few late nights together." She leaned in closely and whispered, *"If you know what I mean."*

Maya knew exactly what she meant. "You and Jamie?"

"Yeah. You could say that he's not interested in just my interior designs." She laughed sexily. "He told me he needed a real woman that knew how to handle him and his lifestyle. Too bad he had to find me in Las Vegas. So far from his home." She looked Maya up and down.

"How long have you and Jamie been seeing each other?"

Gwen shrugged, and waved a hand dismissively. "Oh,

I don't know, for weeks now, I guess. You know, between us girls, it's really just a casual fling." Gwen looked up with a phony smile. "Anyway, I must be going. See you later, Maya. And I guess I'll be seeing Jamie when he gets here on Wednesday. We've got quite a few meetings scheduled to go over the finer details."

Maya watched Gwen saunter down the hallway until she rounded the corner. She was finally able to breathe. *Jamie is sleeping with Gwen?* Not insecure by nature, Maya felt herself shrink in the hallway, as she pressed back against a wall. She caught her breath and stood straight.

While the rational part of her mind was saying, *Pull it together. Talk to Jamie. I'm sure he'll clear all of this up*, the nonrational, but way louder part of her brain was equal parts livid and devastated. *That jerk. I can't believe he is also seeing that awful woman. Why would he do that to me?* Then Maya was hit with a crushing thought. *Am I also a casual fling to him?*

Of course you aren't. He wants to be with you, and you know it! she scolded herself. *Don't be insane.* Gwen was obviously lying. Jamie just wouldn't have had time to be also fooling around with that snake. Maya knew that the little free time that Jamie had, he spent with her. He wouldn't do that to her, anyway. Gwen was jealous. She couldn't have Jamie, so she lied. And that was the most confusing part, she knew Gwen had lied, without a doubt, but she was shocked at how much she felt for Jamie, the power that he held in his hands to crush her so easily.

Maya somehow made her way to her office, walked inside and slumped against the closed door. She closed her eyes and took a deep, calming breath. Then another. *In. And out. In. And out...*

31

JAMIE LET HIMSELF into Maya's apartment with the key she had given him. He was already booked in a suite on the Strip, for convenience of his scheduled meetings, but he knew that he would be spending every night in Maya's bed. Speaking to her on the phone the past few days was strange. She was distant. When he asked her if anything was wrong she gave him an "everything's just fine" that he didn't quite trust. He shook it off, telling himself that the awkwardness came from the distance, and that things would be fine when they were actually together in the same city.

Shutting the door behind him, he inhaled. He could smell her everywhere, and he smiled. Now that he was back with Maya, every day was a relief. He felt lighter and he stayed positive, even when work became too much, he knew that he had Maya. And she was only ever just a phone call away.

He brought his bag to her bedroom and he smiled at the bed, recalling the nights they had spent making love on his last trip. He remembered taking her in the middle of the night, rousing her from her sleep. He couldn't get enough of her. The sound of the door opening interrupted his thoughts. Maya was home.

With a quick stride, he made it to the door to greet her. Upon seeing him, her smile was small. He frowned. "Everything okay?"

"Yeah, everything is fine." She avoided his eyes, and he was unconvinced.

"Are you sure?"

"Yes," she snapped. "I'm fine. How was your flight?"

"Good."

She brushed past him. "Should we go out somewhere for dinner? I'm starved."

He put a hand on the fridge, blocking her from moving any farther away from him. "We aren't going anywhere. Not until you tell me what's going on with you."

She sighed. "Okay. Last week, when Abby was here, I saw Gwen, your interior designer."

"Okay…" He didn't know where she could possibly be going with this. But he knew from the look in her eyes that it certainly wasn't going to be good.

"She told me…"

He was still confused. He narrowed his eyes at her. A look that he knew made most male executives cower. Maya only crossed her arms across her chest in response. "What in the hell did she tell you?"

"That you guys are sleeping together."

Jamie was stunned. "What?"

"Don't be obtuse, Jamie. Why didn't you tell me?"

"There was nothing to tell you. Nothing happened."

"Jamie, she told me—"

"She's lying!"

"Why would she lie about that?"

"Why are we fighting about this? I don't know why

she would lie." He brought his hands to his hair. "I will admit to you that, yeah, there was some flirtation going on. Only over email. And on my last trip here, before we made up, Gwen and I had sort of made plans to hook up. But then I saw you, and I knew that I wouldn't touch her. She came on to me, but I pushed her away. When would I have even had a chance to hook up with her? I haven't been to Vegas since we got back together. What, do you think I've been coming back to Vegas every other day to have sex with her?" He exhaled loudly, frustrated, angry. But when he saw the hurt in her eyes, he forced himself to calm down. He softened. "I don't know why she would tell you that. Maybe to hurt you, to hurt me, but it's not true."

When Maya said nothing, Jamie cupped her face in his large hands.

She looked him in the eyes. "Maybe you should go."

"Maya, don't do this to me again. You have to trust me. If you don't trust me, we won't be able to do this." She still said nothing. "Do you believe me?"

She lowered her head, saying nothing.

He nodded, gathered his bag and quietly left.

32

JAMIE SAT IN his suite, waiting for his next appointment. He didn't like what he was about to do. Gwen was a talented designer, and he loved what she had conceived of for his hotel. But he knew what he had to do. He was livid that she had come between him and Maya, and he hated her for it. He knew that he couldn't stand to be around her just to complete this project, and he would have to find another interior designer. Their contract be damned. Any fee or penalty he incurred, he was prepared to pay it to remove Gwen from the project. His relationship with Maya was worth more than money, or even the shot to his reputation.

When her knock sounded at the door, he stood. He opened it, and Gwen brushed past him, coming close enough that he could feel her heat through his clothing.

"Hello, Jamie, how are you?" She sat at the table and looked up through sultry eyelashes. She opened the folder she held. "You should see what I came up with for the pool area."

"I'm fine, Gwen." He cleared his throat. "And there's no need to take that out."

She looked at him, puzzled.

"I know that you spoke to Maya."

Her face went pale.

"I know that you told her that we slept together. Why did you tell her that?"

"Jamie, I know that it's only a matter of time until we get together." She stood and put her hands on his chest. "I know that you want to be with me. Nobody rejects me."

Jamie clasped her wrists in his hands. "Gwen, don't embarrass yourself. You found out that Maya and I were together and you lashed out because I wasn't interested in you. So really, Gwen, all that's left to say is that I called you here to tell you that I will no longer be needing your services for Swerve."

"Jamie, don't be ridiculous."

"I'm being serious. We're done."

"Don't think you'll be able to use my designs—"

"I don't want them. I don't want anything having to do with you. You cost me the woman I love and I don't want you anywhere near me, her or my hotel."

Gwen straightened, hurt pride and fire in her eyes. "Fine, Jamie, have it your way. I'm leaving. But don't forget, I know a lot of influential people in this city, and don't think I will speak kindly of you."

"I don't need anything from you, Gwen, especially your recommendation. I'll do just fine on my own."

Gwen huffed, stalked to the door and slammed it on her way out.

So, THAT LEFT Jamie back where he started—handling all of the building details of his hotel, and he still had no assistant. He sighed as he walked into Garrett Collins's office. He was ready to admit that he needed the man's help. He was in over his head, and the most immediate of problems was that he needed to find a new interior designer. He had lucked out when Garrett had introduced him to Gwen, but he obviously couldn't keep working with her.

Some days later, Maya still wouldn't talk to him. He hadn't told her that he fired Gwen. He wondered if the Gwen situation was the only reason she had forced him away. But he didn't have time to worry about it at the moment.

"What can I do for you, Jamie?" Garrett smiled at the younger man, brushing aside the papers he had in front of him.

"Well, this is kind of embarrassing, Garrett. But I'm afraid I need a little help. And it pains me to have to come to you, but I'm a desperate man," he said humbly.

"Jamie, asking for help should never be an embarrassment," the older man chided him. "But to come to me like this, you must really need some assistance. What's on your mind?"

Jamie looked at his hands. "Well, I need to find another interior designer. Gwen didn't quite work out."

Garrett furrowed his brow in confusion. "Huh. That's surprising. Gwen is one of my most trusted advisors. Dare I ask what happened?"

"She did a great job, Garrett. But she can't continue to work for me. It's personal, I'm afraid."

"Ah, I see. Does this have anything to do with Maya?"

"Maya?" Jamie was startled. He didn't think that Garrett knew anything about their relationship or their problems.

"I'm not stupid, son. I see the way you look at each

other. I'm in the business of people, Jamie. I have been for a long time. Want to tell me what's troubling you?"

"This is awkward to talk about, sir, but Gwen insinuated herself into our relationship, she lied to Maya about the status of what had been a strictly professional relationship." Jamie put a hand on the other man's desk. "I don't want to disparage her work. She did an excellent job for me, but I can't use her now."

"I understand."

"So I was wondering if you knew anyone who could come aboard for my hotel this late in the game?"

"You're asking for my connections?"

Jamie bowed his head. He hated having to come to anyone for help. "Sir, I wouldn't be here if I didn't need help."

"I know that must have been hard for you to admit. But I'll gladly help you, Jamie. You're a good man. And you're a fantastic businessman. I see a lot of myself in you. I can't wait to see the finished result of all your hard work, and I actually look forward to you being one of my most formidable competitors here on the Strip." He rolled up his sleeves. "I like a good challenge, and I think you'll provide me with one."

Jamie blushed and lowered his head again. No one in his life, besides Dr. C., had ever spoken to him with such pride and doled out such praise. "Thank you, sir. I look forward to it, as well."

Garrett pulled out a drawer and rifled through a box of business cards. He pulled out one and scrawled a phone number on the back. "Kurt Stanfield. He is great at what he does and I guarantee he won't try to get in your pants," he chuckled. "Call his personal number on the back and tell him I gave it to you. He owes me a favor."

Jamie stood. "Thank you so much, Garrett. I really owe you one."

Garrett waved a hand. "You owe me nothing, kid. But I expect you to keep our girl happy. She's been pining around here for the past couple of days. I don't like to see that."

He grimaced that Maya was hurt. "I'm working on it. I'm going to make it right."

"I hope so, for both of your sakes."

33

MAYA WAS IN her kitchen when her phone rang. She ran to it and saw Jamie's number displayed on the screen. She frowned, debating whether or not to answer it. She had stubbornly refused to take any of his calls in the month that had passed since she had spoken to him, although it felt like an eternity, and thinking about Jamie still hurt her. That was a sure sign that they shouldn't be together. He had too much power to cause her pain. She couldn't risk her heart with him, because he would surely break it.

Sure, Abby had said she was being stupid. *Not being able to live without him is the surest sign that you should be together*, she'd advised her. Abby had told her that this was just another way she pushed away her happiness. Maya had sabotaged her own relationship, and Gwen had given her the perfect excuse to do it. She didn't see it that way, and she had done well to avoid him at all costs in the past few miserable weeks, but still, she finally answered his call.

"Hello?"

"Maya," he said. It was barely audible. "Thanks for answering. It's good to hear your voice."

"Why did you call me?" she asked him, her eyes closed.

"I'll explain later. But there's a car outside your building. I need you to get in it."

"Jamie, what's going on?"

"Just trust me, okay? Get in the car." She didn't say anything. She could hear his frustration from his end of the line. "Maya, please."

She sighed. Not from impatience but from the painful way he made her chest clench. "Okay, I'll get in the car. Where is it going to take me?"

"Don't worry about that."

"Jamie—"

"Trust me."

"Okay."

WHEN THE TOWN car stopped, she found herself outside of the very-soon-to-be-open Swerve Hotel and Nightclub. She thanked the driver as he helped her out and she walked to the front door. She pulled on the handle to find that it was unlocked. She walked inside and was blown away by the hotel's lobby. It was sleek and modern, in shades of white and charcoal. She glanced around, looking for Jamie. And she saw him, as he entered the room from what she imagined was the restaurant.

He stopped when he saw her. He was the same gorgeous man that she had left just a month ago. He wasn't quite as polished as she had seen him in the past. His suit was slightly rumpled and it looked as if he had skipped a few of his weekly barber appointments, as told by the hair that had began to curl around his ears and at his collar. He had also not shaved for a couple of days, at least. The makings of a beard a marked his face. But it was his eyes that she found the most striking about him. They were normally a lively, vibrant blue, but they had dulled since she'd last seen him, and her heart broke for him. She had abandoned him when he needed her. He was embarking on one of the most important and stressful ventures in his life, and she had left him.

Jamie came to her. "Thanks for coming. You look beautiful."

She looked down at her outfit. He had caught her cooking, and she was wearing an old tank top and a pair of yoga pants. "In this?"

"In anything."

She smiled. "This place looks amazing, Jamie. I'm really proud of you."

"Thanks." He also took an appreciative look around. "I'm really proud of it, as well."

"How is the Montreal hotel doing?"

"Great, actually. Out-performing in every way."

Maya shook her head in wonder. Jamie could do anything that he put his mind to. "That's fantastic. I'm really happy for you. And I know that this place is going to be even more successful. You've got everything."

"Almost," he said, with a sad smile. "Would you like a tour?" he asked her, extending his hand.

"I would." She took his hand in her own.

AFTER JAMIE HAD walked her around the property, which housed the hotel and nightclub, showing her the facilities, the amenities, the restaurant and a performance venue, they had moved on to one of the guest suites. Jamie merely opened the door, and neither had made a move to go inside, as if the presence of a bed would rip apart any resolve that either of them were holding on to. Maya was relieved; if she had gotten Jamie near one of those beds, she would have surely been tempted to tear off his clothes and push him to the bed.

When they returned to the lobby, she headed for the door, but Jamie pulled at her arm. "Maya, wait."

She stopped and turned to him.

He took her hands, covering them with his much larger ones. "What happened to us?"

What *had* happened? They were doing so well as a couple. Sure, the distance was hard, but not impossible. Maya had agonized over why she had acted the way she had. In the end, she believed that Abby was right about her. She had known that she was falling in love with Jamie, and that had scared her. Gwen had just provided a convenient way out; a convenient way to get indignantly mad at Jamie and make him out to be the bad guy. She had pushed him away. She had to hurt Jamie before he had the chance to hurt her.

"The CliffsNotes version? I was hurt when you didn't disclose the relationship you had with Gwen."

"Dammit, me and Gwen weren't in a relationship. We never slept together. And when I made those plans to meet up with her, you and I certainly weren't together. You moved to another goddamn country to get away from me."

"I know, and I know that she lied to hurt both of us. But I realized that my feelings were hurt and it was then that I realized that I had given you way too much power over my emotions. You owned my heart and only you had the power to break it. It scared me. I'm afraid to get hurt. I loved you too much and not being with you broke my heart. Abby said that I was being stupid and I should go to you—"

"I knew I liked her for a reason."

"She's pretty great. She told me that I should be with the person I can't live without. And that's you, Jamie." She smiled at him, allowing a tear to cascade down her cheek. "I'm in love with you."

He brought his fingertips to her face to catch the teardrop. Her cheek was still as smooth as he remembered it being. "I love you, too, Maya. You can trust me with your heart. I can do anything I want in business, but it really doesn't mean anything if you aren't with me."

He pulled her in to kiss her deeply. She finally felt whole again. Like some giant part that was missing from her had returned. She kissed him back. Being with Jamie, this felt right.

34

"So, this is it." Trevor raised his champagne glass to Jamie. "The day you've been working for your entire career."

One week later, Jamie, Maya, Trevor and Abby were inside Jamie's office in the newest and most hotly anticipated resort on Las Vegas Boulevard. The grand opening party was about to start, and the three had decided that Jamie should have a much-needed respite from the chaos that had followed him for weeks. Trevor ordered a very nice bottle of champagne, and Maya had brought in trays of Jamie's favorite snacks. Maya and Abby also raised their glasses in Jamie's direction, and Trevor continued his toast.

"To Jamie Sellers and the next step of his global domination of good times. To the international expansion of Swerve Hotels! From Montreal to Vegas. But where next? Amsterdam? Ibiza? Bangkok?"

"Hear, hear," Maya chimed in, taking a sip.

Jamie smiled and draped an arm around Maya's waist and he pulled her closer. "Thanks, guys, for all of this. It's really great. But I wouldn't have been able to do any of this without the three of you in this room. Trevor, you've been with me since the beginning. You're my sounding board, you keep me grounded. You work your ass off, managing my business." He turned to Abby.

"And, Abby, I don't know you very well, but you brought Maya into my life and talked some sense into her when she was headed back out, so for that I owe you. And, Maya." He put his glass down and turned to face her. "Maya, I love you. I think I've loved you since that night you kissed me, and not being with you has been the most awful feeling I've ever experienced. But right now—" he dropped to his knee in front of her, and somewhere in the background he heard Abby gasp "—Maya, I want to be with you forever. Here, or in Montreal, it doesn't matter." He reached into his pocket and pulled out a small, square box. "Maya, marry me. Please."

The sheen of tears covering Maya's eyes finally gave way and they streamed down her face. She fell to her knees so she could face him. "You jerk," she sniffed. "I'm ruining my makeup before the party. This took a lot of work, you know." They laughed together. "But I'll marry you. I'd have to be a fool not to. I love you, Jamie. Yes." Any other words she was about to say were stolen from her lips as he pulled her in and kissed her.

After a while Trevor finally cleared his throat. "Guys, I hate to break this up, but is there any way we can get in there to congratulate you guys before we head down to the party." He looked at his watch. "Also, we're going to be late."

Jamie stood and helped Maya to her feet. "I don't really care."

Jamie had never felt love or support like this before in his life. He had a group of friends, and the woman who owned his heart. The people at the party would have to wait.

As Abby and Maya embraced in celebration, Trevor pulled Jamie into a strong bro-hug. "This is your night, guy. Go get 'em. It's going to be a great night."

As they broke apart, Jamie searched for Maya's hand, and the foursome walked to the door to head down to the party that would soon start. Yeah, it was going to be a great night. He had everything he had ever wanted.

* * * * *

REQUEST YOUR FREE BOOKS!
2 FREE NOVELS PLUS 2 FREE GIFTS!

H HARLEQUIN®

Blaze

red-hot reads!

YES! Please send me 2 FREE Harlequin® Blaze® novels and my 2 FREE gifts (gifts are worth about $10). After receiving them, if I don't wish to receive any more books, I can return the shipping statement marked "cancel." If I don't cancel, I will receive 4 brand-new novels every month and be billed just $4.74 per book in the U.S. or $5.21 per book in Canada. That's a savings of at least 14% off the cover price. It's quite a bargain. Shipping and handling is just 50¢ per book in the U.S. and 75¢ per book in Canada.* I understand that accepting the 2 free books and gifts places me under no obligation to buy anything. I can always return a shipment and cancel at any time. Even if I never buy another book, the two free books and gifts are mine to keep forever.

150/350 HDN GH2D

Name _____ (PLEASE PRINT)

Address _____ Apt. #

City _____ State/Prov. _____ Zip/Postal Code

Signature (if under 18, a parent or guardian must sign)

Mail to the **Reader Service:**
IN U.S.A.: P.O. Box 1867, Buffalo, NY 14240-1867
IN CANADA: P.O. Box 609, Fort Erie, Ontario L2A 5X3

**Want to try two free books from another line?
Call 1-800-873-8635 or visit www.ReaderService.com.**

* Terms and prices subject to change without notice. Prices do not include applicable taxes. Sales tax applicable in N.Y. Canadian residents will be charged applicable taxes. Offer not valid in Quebec. This offer is limited to one order per household. Not valid for current subscribers to Harlequin Blaze books. All orders subject to credit approval. Credit or debit balances in a customer's account(s) may be offset by any other outstanding balance owed by or to the customer. Please allow 4 to 6 weeks for delivery. Offer available while quantities last.

Your Privacy—The Reader Service is committed to protecting your privacy. Our Privacy Policy is available online at www.ReaderService.com or upon request from the Reader Service.

We make a portion of our mailing list available to reputable third parties that offer products we believe may interest you. If you prefer that we not exchange your name with third parties, or if you wish to clarify or modify your communication preferences, please visit us at www.ReaderService.com/consumerschoice or write to us at Reader Service Preference Service, P.O. Box 9062, Buffalo, NY 14240-9062. Include your complete name and address.

HB15

*Liam Magee is at the ranch for a wedding—so is
Hope Caldwell, who he's wanted in his bed for months.
Hope craves the sexy cowboy, but can she trust him
for more than a fling?*

*Read on for a sneak preview of
COWBOY AFTER DARK, the second story of 2016 in
Vicki Lewis Thompson's sexy cowboy saga
THUNDER MOUNTAIN BROTHERHOOD.*

Hope was a puzzle, and he didn't have all the pieces
yet. Something didn't fit the picture she was presenting
to everyone, but he'd figure out the mystery eventually.
Right now they had a soft blanket waiting. He lifted her
down and led her over to it.

He'd ground-tied both Navarre and Isabeau, who were
old and extremely mellow. The horses weren't going
anywhere. Hope sat on the blanket like a person about
to have a picnic, except they hadn't brought anything to
eat or drink.

Liam decided to set the tone. After relaxing beside
her, he took off his Stetson and stretched out on his back.
"You can see the stars a lot better if you lie back."

To his surprise, she laughed. "Is that a maneuver?"

"A maneuver?"

"You know, a move."

"Oh. I guess it's a move, now that you mention it." He
sighed. "The truth is, I want to kiss you, and it'll be easier
if you're down here instead of up there."

"So it has nothing to do with looking at the stars."

"It has everything to do with looking at the stars! First you lie on your back and appreciate how beautiful they are, and then I get to kiss you underneath their brilliant light. It all goes together."

"You sound cranky."

"That's because nobody has ever made me break it down."

"I see." She flopped down onto the blanket. "Beautiful stars. Now kiss me."

"You just completely destroyed the mood."

"Are you sure?" She rolled to her side and reached over to run a finger down his tense jaw. "Last time I checked, we still had a canopy of stars arching over us."

"A canopy of stars." He turned to face her and propped his head on his hand. "Did you write that?"

"None of your beeswax."

Although she'd said it in a teasing way, he got the message. No more questions about her late great writing career. "Let's start over. How about if you lie back and look up at the stars?"

"I did that already, and you didn't pick up your cue."

"Try it again."

She sighed and rolled to her back. "Beautiful stars. Now kiss—"

His mouth covered hers before she could finish.

Don't miss COWBOY AFTER DARK
by Vicki Lewis Thompson.
Available in July 2016 wherever
Harlequin® Blaze® books and ebooks are sold.

www.Harlequin.com

HBEXP0616

Reading Has Its Rewards

Earn **FREE BOOKS!**

Register at **Harlequin My Rewards** and submit your Harlequin purchases from wherever you shop to earn points for free books and other exclusive rewards.

Plus submit your purchases from now till May 30th for a chance to win a $500 Visa Card*.

Visit **HarlequinMyRewards.com** today

Earn **FREE** REWARDS Join Today! HarlequinMyRewards.com

MYR16R1